RISEN GODS

A DARK FANTASY SUPERNATURAL THRILLER

J. F. PENN & J. THORN

Risen Gods
Copyright © J.F.Penn and J. Thorn (2015). All rights reserved.

www.JFPenn.com
www.JThorn.net

ISBN: 978-1-912105-22-9

Requests to publish work from this book should be sent to:
joanna@CurlUpPress.com

Cover and Interior Design: JD Smith Design
Map of Aotearoa, New Zealand: Brianne Ryan

Printed by Lightning Source

www.CurlUpPress.com

From J.F.Penn: Dedicated to Nicky and Tim,
Anna and Angus Raeburn.

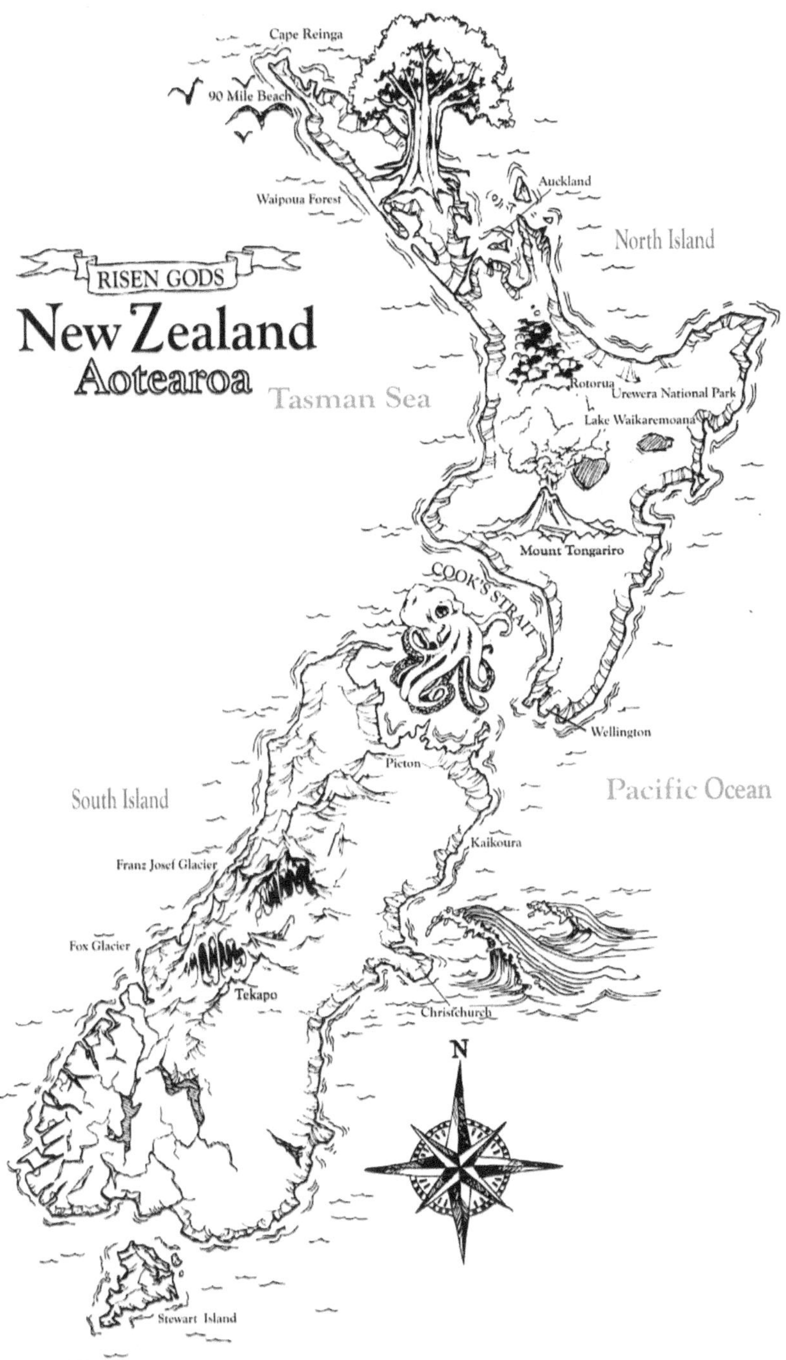

RISEN GODS
New Zealand
Aotearoa
Tasman Sea
North Island
South Island
Pacific Ocean
Cape Reinga
90 Mile Beach
Waipoua Forest
Auckland
Rotorua
Urewera National Park
Lake Waikaremoana
Mount Tongariro
COOK'S STRAIT
Wellington
Picton
Kaikoura
Franz Josef Glacier
Fox Glacier
Tekapo
Christchurch
Stewart Island
N

PROLOGUE

IN THE TIME BEFORE, Ranginui, god of the sky, and Papatuanuku, goddess of the earth, were joined together in their love. This was the time of Te Po, the Great Nights of Coming into Being.

But the sons of the gods could not flourish within the tight embrace of their parents.

So the children thrust them apart.

Ranginui's blood stained the skies of the west and Papatuanuku's blood dripped to the ground, forming red ochre. The tears of their grief became the rain and the mist.

The brothers fought amongst themselves and their wrath shook the earth. Until finally, the gods of the rivers and the mountains were still and silent.

For a time, it was quiet.

But now, the gods of Aotearoa are rising again.

CHAPTER 1

A SUDDEN GUST OF wind blew and Ben Henare tightened the guide rope, pulling the sail inwards to catch the draught. The Moth-class dinghy lifted up onto its foils, hydroplaning across the top of the waves. Ben laughed aloud at the sensation of flying, and leaned back to catch even more wind. This was where he felt most alive, out here on the ocean with the sun sparkling on the water. There were moments when he could even forget what lay back on the shore. Out here, nothing mattered except these moments of bliss.

The gust shifted and the Moth dropped back into the water. His speed dropped off and Ben scanned the ocean for the next patch of wind, his eyes alert for the particular ruffle of waves that indicated the breeze to come.

A whoop of joy came from behind him. Ben

turned his head to see Lucy planing across the turquoise ocean, flying above the waves. Her freckled face beamed with sheer delight.

"Quit sitting around, Henare!" she shouted as she zoomed past. Her bright blue eyes reflected the water and the sky above. Her thick plait of blonde hair trailed over her shoulder, soaked by the sea spray.

Ben grinned and pulled his sail in again, picking up speed as he followed, but he couldn't catch her this time. She whipped around, tacking hard and headed back towards him.

He raced to meet her, a direct course that must surely end in their collision.

But at the last minute, they both pulled away slightly, neither giving ground. They laughed, both still loving the game they had played since childhood.

The ocean had always been their playground, ever since they had met at the Pegasus Bay Sailing Club at nine years old. Ben's father, Ropata, worked maintenance at the boatyard, his weathered hands rough from sandpaper and stained with varnish. Lucy's father owned the place; his hands were always smooth and unmarked. Hands that knew money, Ben's father said, but not the smooth grain of a wooden deck.

Perhaps it was true that the Pakeha, the white New Zealanders, had lost touch with the natural world. Many said that even the *tangata whenua*, the Maori people of the land, were losing that connection, preferring the good life in the city to the inherent hardship of wild forests and mountains. But their love for the ocean transcended their disparate backgrounds and out here, Ben and Lucy were equal.

Well, almost equal, Ben thought to himself.

Sometimes he had to admit that Lucy might be the better sailor. How she managed to keep her skills up while she trained to be a doctor, he didn't know. He was just grateful that she could make time for sailing with him on her holiday break from University. Not that he was getting a break. His work in the boatyard only increased in the summer months, especially with his father's diabetes getting worse. But on the days he could escape, there was nowhere else he'd rather be.

And no one else he'd rather be here with.

The strong wind dropped and they sailed alongside each other in the gentle breeze. Ben could hear the slap of waves on the hull, the call of the gulls above. The sun was a blessing, a perfect edge of warmth to the cool spray of the sea. He breathed in deeply, letting the smell of the ocean calm his mind, trying to fix this moment in his memory.

He looked back towards the shore, past Lucy's boat to the coastline beyond. The long spit of New Brighton jutted south towards the Lyttelton peninsula and, behind it, the city of Christchurch. Most of the houses had been rebuilt after the earthquakes that shook the city in 2011, but many people who had left had not returned. Those who did remain were stronger, more resilient now, but they had not forgotten.

A sharp, icy wind cut through the air and Ben let out the sail in surprise at the temperature shift. He looked up and frowned. The sky darkened as thick black clouds loomed above. Summer storms weren't unusual, but there had been nothing on the weather radar before they'd come out.

Lucy tacked and came alongside, letting out her sail to slow the boat. A deep frown marred her natural features, her blue eyes sharp with focus.

"We should go back in," she called across the short distance between them. Then her eyes widened as she looked beyond Ben to the horizon. "We have to go *now*."

Ben turned and his breath was sucked from him, heart pounding as he saw what came towards them.

A wave towered where the ocean met the sky.

Even this far away, it was gigantic – a tidal wave like the one that had ruined the city years before. The sky above swirled with storm clouds. Tendrils of darkness crept ever closer as a wall of water raced towards them.

"Now, Ben." Lucy's voice was urgent. "We can still make it back before it hits."

Ben turned and met her eyes. There was so much he wanted to say. He prayed there would still be a chance to say it.

"Be safe," he said. She nodded, her mouth tightening as she looked east towards the approaching wave.

"I'll see you back home," Lucy said and pulled her sail taut, racing away towards the shore.

Ben followed her lead, fighting for control of the boat as the wind howled about him and the waves began to rise. Rain hammered down and needles of freezing water slammed into him.

A flash of lightning split the sky, and a deafening roll of thunder filled the air.

The tiny Moth dinghies were like flotsam as the storm grew in intensity, the waves soon over two meters high. Ben lost sight of Lucy but there was nothing he could do. He fought to keep his own boat heading back towards shore.

A huge wave rolled beneath him. One moment

he was down in a trough looking up at the walls of water either side, and then he was up on the crest.

He couldn't help himself.

Ben looked back towards the eastern horizon. The giant tidal wave was closer now. There was no way to outrun it.

A calm descended upon him. The sea had called to him all his life; perhaps it was right that he would end it here. Ben was transfixed by the power of the wave. In that moment, he stared into the heart of the sea. His pulse raced as he faced the onslaught.

Words spoken by his grandfather came to his lips – a prayer to Tangaroa, the god of the sea. A *karakia* from the old times, the fishermen's ritual chant for protection.

The words changed something in Ben's perception. The wave shimmered, and he saw beyond the towering water to the horror beneath. The tentacles of a huge creature writhed within the wave, thick ropes of powerful muscle tipped with barbed hooks that could rip flesh and peel skin off its prey. Ben could feel its rage, its need to feast as its huge dark eye bore into him. Then, it turned back into the deep and the wave rolled on.

He saw the wreck of a ship within the water, rotten bodies still hanging from its spars, the eyes of the corpses eaten by denizens of the deep. The smell of the long dead rolled from the wave, mingled with the rank stench of rotten fish. There was a flash of silver within the surge as a gigantic ball of fish broke the surface, forced by the upwelling. The ball was broken apart by the thrust of a great white shark, its rows of teeth slashing at the feast.

Ben thought he heard his grandfather's voice calling to him across the ocean, telling him to keep going, to trust in his skill as a sailor. His grandfather Tamati was a *kaumatua*, one of the elders, a wise man who still held to the old ways. Perhaps they were the only ways left to trust in now.

Ben sent out a prayer for Lucy, asking Tangaroa to keep her safe. Then, he tightened the sail and leaned out into the storm, bracing his legs and swinging out on the trapeze over the water. The Moth planed across the tips of the roiling waves beneath. He turned the bow south towards the Akaroa peninsula. It was his best chance. If he could sail fast across the face of the storm, he could find shelter in one of the bays south of Lyttelton.

Ben aimed for the shore, desperate to reach it as the rain hammered him and the salt waves threatened to pull him from the boat and crush him to the depths.

Then, the eye of the storm was upon him.

For a moment, he soared with the power of the

wind and the Moth lifted clear off the waves. He really was flying. The detail of the shoreline came into focus. If he could hold on for just a few more minutes, he might make it to shelter before the tidal wave hit.

The boat plummeted back to the waves. The jolt shook Ben from the deck.

He tumbled into the freezing sea, flailing to catch hold of the Moth's guide rope, but it was ripped away from him.

The boat spun in the water. The boom swung, smacking Ben's head.

Pain lanced through him. The cold ocean pierced his padded life jacket. The grey green of the monstrous wave loomed above him as Ben sank into the black.

CHAPTER 2

LUCY TOOK A DEEP breath, her eyes fixed on the coastline as it loomed ever closer. The concrete of the pier and the hard edges of the buildings were suddenly a threat, not a haven. As a junior doctor, she had seen the impact on a human body up close. She could almost feel the pain of the crush as it sped towards her.

Time slowed as she rode the crest of the wave. In the roar of the storm, Lucy became part of the water and the wind, all her years of sailing experience distilled into this moment. She didn't think of Ben or her family or the thousands of people in the city before her about to be torn asunder. She only thought of adjusting the sail to the wild wind and surviving the next second.

She felt the salt spray of the chasing wave on her neck, the freezing embrace of the water reaching for her. For a moment, she wanted to relax into the elemental, to sink into the depths. Only pain lay ahead.

But the Campions didn't give up.

Her family had been among the first white settlers in New Zealand, hardy men and women who worked to tame the natural world. If it were fighting back, Lucy would not go down peacefully.

The wave rushed towards the shore as she wrestled to stay with it. She rode the crest, the Moth flying with the power of the wind. Lucy scanned the approaching shore, summoning the calm she often did in the hospital when things spun out of control. She couldn't fight the situation, only try to ride it out and stay alive.

The spit of New Brighton jutted south, protecting an estuary beyond from the power of the ocean. Her house was further up, but at Southshore the land was only one street wide and then the mangroves began. Lucy angled the Moth across the face of the wave towards the gap.

If she could just–

Her thought was cut off as a wave hit the starboard side. The tiller was wrenched from Lucy's hand. The boat tipped and she lost control.

She plummeted into the water, cold freezing the breath in her lungs. She clawed her way for what she thought was the surface, eyes open as she searched for the light above.

But the waters swirled around, cloaking her.

She didn't know which way was up.

Panic rose within her chest, squeezing her heart. She could hear the thump of her pulse in her ears.

Something bashed into her side. Pain lanced through her as the broken Moth whirled in the water. There was no hope now, no question – Lucy knew that she would die here alone.

She sent Ben her love, hoping that he would make it. He would never know what he meant to her now, for even as their lives had taken different directions, he was as much a part of her as the ocean was.

With that thought, she stopped fighting, letting the column of water propel her towards the shore.

As the final bubble of air left her mouth, the wave crashed down.

Lucy tumbled and rolled in the water but this time, instinct drove her towards the surface. Her leg smashed into something but the pain only helped her focus as she pulled herself upwards.

Sound returned in a rush as she broke the surface, waves churning about her. She gasped for breath as she trod water with her good leg, crying with relief.

Lucy looked around, trying to get her bearings. Somehow, she had made it into the estuary and the waves had pushed her into the shallower northern end.

To the west, the wave was dipping, losing power as it moved inland. Regardless, it would crush the city of Christchurch within minutes.

To the east, the spit of New Brighton. The houses on the southern tip were mostly underwater, the trees crushed and bent. She could see people clambering onto roofs to escape the swelling water. The houses to the north were still standing, but even from here she could see the destruction.

The *chop chop* of a helicopter made Lucy look up. She thought about waving her arms but she knew they would have more urgent cases than picking her out of the estuary.

She was so tired, so cold. She could just lie back here in the water. Surely someone would come eventually.

The doctor inside her noted the beginnings of shock setting in. This was not a normal day. No one would come for her.

If she stayed here, she would die.

Lucy began to swim towards the shore, heading for home. Earlier that day, she had waved to her mum in the kitchen as she'd left to go sailing with Ben. She had kissed her father's bald head and he had grunted his goodbye, focused on the morning's paper. Her little sister Amber hadn't emerged from her teenage den, sleeping in like most fourteen-year-olds on a weekend. Since leaving for Uni, Lucy actually felt more charitable towards her, despite how much they used to fight when she was at home.

And then there was Ben.

She sent out a positive thought to him, willing him to survive. With every stroke towards the shore, Lucy whispered the names of those she loved as a mantra to keep her going.

It seemed like an age to get to the shoreline, but it was probably more like ten minutes. Lucy pulled herself up onto the pebbled beach, panting with the effort. It was eerily quiet, as if the world waited for permission to respond to the disaster.

The quiet after the storm, and before the aftermath.

She should get to the hospital. They would need all hands on deck. Lucy shivered. First she had to get home, check on her family and get some dry clothes. Her leg throbbed, but she couldn't tend to it yet. She ignored the pain and struggled to her feet, taking an inventory of her physical state. Aches, bruises, battered, cut, but not broken.

She limped down the road, away from the estuary and into the streets that led into what had been the pretty suburb of New Brighton only a few hours ago.

Now it was a ruin.

The first house she came to looked like it had been stomped on by a giant. The ground floor had been pulverized into timber slivers and loose bricks, shaken and torn apart. The roof hung inches from the ground at a sharp angle. An old woman clawed at the bricks, tears running down her face.

"Please help me," she called out to Lucy, her face a mask of agony. "My husband, he's in there."

Lucy felt a wave of empathy for the woman, but she knew she had to get to her own family. There was no way the man was alive in there. Nothing could be done for him.

As she walked on through the streets, the devastation only worsened.

The sound of children crying, the pained screams of the injured and the barking and howling of dogs filled the air. A man sat in the rubble of his yard, the body of a young girl on his lap. He rocked her, his eyes fixed on the sky above. A couple huddled together on the edge of their property, a deep fissure splitting it open between them. They stared into the darkness, seemingly unable to move.

One house had all its panes of glass still miraculously intact, but the entire brickwork had crumbled, the house collapsing in on itself. Another building had lost one whole side, leaving the rooms open to the elements. Lucy could see bookshelves and a bed inside, but no people.

There were bodies, too. Crushed and broken, ruined by a force of nature no one had seen coming despite the alarms put in place after the last disaster. New Zealand had ever been God's Own Country. Was it now forsaken?

Those she passed called for help, but Lucy kept her eyes fixed forward, a sense of foreboding growing in the pit of her stomach as she approached her own street.

The sight was no different than what she had already seen, but this time it was her world that had crumbled. The house she had played in, the home she had grown up in, was now a ruin.

Ignoring the pain in her leg, Lucy ran up the street, tears blurring her vision.

The road had buckled and the tarmac split. Steam poured out of the cleft. Her dad's Volvo had fallen sideways, crushed into the hole in the earth, the metal crunched flat. The force of the water had come at an angle, shearing the roof of the house off on impact. The debris had landed on the house next door, flattening their garage. The window where her mum had waved goodbye was gone, along with that whole side of the building. It lay in blocks of brick and plaster now, dashed into its component parts.

"Mum! Dad!" Lucy called in desperation as she reached the gate. "Amber!"

She tried to keep herself from sobbing. She had to search for them.

They might be OK.

They had to be OK.

She picked her way through the rubble towards the back of the house, careful to avoid the deep holes that now peppered the yard. The air smelled of sewage and escaped gas and a pervasive salty damp where the ocean encroached into the human realm.

The back door of the house stood open, and Lucy felt a surge of hope. They had been taught since they were little to get under a doorframe. Maybe her family huddled inside.

She pushed the door open and stepped in, her eyes widening at what she saw.

CHAPTER 3

BEN WOKE TO AGONIZED screams. For a moment, he couldn't tell whether he was dead or alive. The anguish and pain in those voices made him feel as though he were in his people's underworld, deep within Rarohenga.

A sharp pain in his thigh forced his eyes open. He brushed the sand from his leg, where a deep gash oozed dark red blood. Ben winced, the saltwater searing the wound as he sat up. His dark hair was matted and stiff with salt. He blinked as blurry shapes ran past him on the shore, but as he rubbed his eyes, his vision began to clear.

The beach in front of him was littered with the wreckage of the storm. A few meters away, a man huddled over the body of a woman on the sand, surf churning around him. A splintered hunk of wood slid up the sand and nudged the corpse. The man moaned in despair, clutching her to his chest.

There were more bodies in the surf, angry water pushing and pulling them in a macabre dance of the dead. Ben wanted to go and pull them to shore, but there were so many. Shingles and pieces of what used to be homes stuck out of the sand, smashed into splinters on the hard-packed shoreline. An old Volkswagen was perched atop a fifteen-foot fishing boat that had capsized and now sank, buried slowly by the tide.

Ben clutched his leg and did his best to ignore the pain. His head pounded, but at least the blood had slowed to a trickle. He moved his hands over the rest of his body and felt no other pain. He had survived.

Lucy, he thought. *Did she make it?*

He couldn't even consider that she hadn't. She was a survivor.

Sirens wailed in the distance, followed by a series of short explosions. He had to move. He had to get to his father. Ben stood and took a step, wincing at the pain in his leg, but he stumbled on. He was in better shape than the corpses that bobbed in the surf.

He turned his back on the ocean and looked west. The mountains loomed in the distance beneath blackened clouds. Closer to him, smoke rose over the city, spires of black haze climbing into the sky.

Christchurch had been hit again.

Ben orientated himself to the surroundings. He was on a beach near Pigeon Bay, looking across the tip of Godley Beach State Park towards the city. The tidal wave had left behind a wall of debris, blocking the only road from Pigeon Bay to Diamond Harbor. He picked his way through the rubble and followed the road regardless. There was no other way back to the city.

Back to his father … and Lucy.

But Ben sensed something else, something more primitive – more *powerful*. He felt his grandfather call out. The man was in trouble. He needed Ben's help. Soon.

Ben pushed away the pain and started to jog. The increased oxygen lifted the fog in his head. He couldn't think about Lucy. They had been on the water with no identification, no phone, no money. Even if he had his phone, Ben doubted service would still be operational. After the last disaster, the lines had been swamped and it had been impossible to reach people.

He took a deep breath and pinched at the cramp now blossoming in his side. He needed water and, despite the destruction, his stomach rumbled.

I should go south, he thought. *There's no way to get to Dad in Christchurch. Grandfather will know what to do.*

He stopped and turned to face southwest, towards Tekapo. It would take days to reach his grandfather's place on foot. He needed a vehicle. If he got further away from the shoreline, there might be some areas untouched by the wave. Ben walked further into the maze of debris left behind.

He emerged from one street to see a couple huddled on the side of the road. They tended to a wounded child between them. The little boy wept in agony and, even from a distance, Ben could see his leg was twisted out of shape. Ben's years of first aid training at the boathouse would come in handy now. He jogged over to help.

As he reached the roadside, he noticed a group of teenagers gathered together, loitering and watching the scene. Then the air shifted around them.

Thin, black smoke curled up from the ground. It wound around the legs of the group like a semi-transparent, fast growing vine. Tendrils crawled up their bodies to their heads and then billowed out. With every breath, the boys inhaled the darkness.

What the hell?

They turned as one to face Ben, expressions blank, dark eyes shadowed as curls of smoke clung to their skin. They took a step towards him, cutting off his path to the injured child.

A woman stumbled from a house across the street. The boys turned in unison at the sound and a tall, lanky boy, their leader, approached her in two long strides. He grabbed the woman by the arm, holding her while the others formed a circle around them both. The woman screamed and tried to pull away but the boys closed ranks, grasping hands reaching for her clothes.

Ben ran towards them, leaping over rocks and other debris.

"Hey, leave her alone," he shouted.

The tall, lanky boy turned at Ben's approach and pulled a knife from his belt, hefting its weight.

"She's ours. Go find your own."

"Get away from her," Ben said with a step forward. "She's not for you."

The boy's eyes rolled back in his head. Ben could have sworn he saw the black smoke inside them. A deep laugh rumbled from him, a voice that couldn't possibly belong to this body.

The circle of boys all turned to face Ben. The woman seized her opportunity and bolted from inside the circle, running off down the road. They ignored her, focused on Ben now. They drew their weapons – knives, pipes, cricket bats and rocks.

Ben took a step back, his eyes fixed on the boys. He had one chance to run. If he fell, they would be on him.

He saw the lanky boy's eyes narrow, his hand clenched on the knife handle.

Ben turned and ran. The boys roared as one, their footsteps thunderous on the cracked pavement as they dashed after him. Ben darted down a side road, zigzagging where he could.

But he was tiring.

The boys whooped at the thrill of the chase, the primal sound of hunters closing in on their prey.

Ben ducked down another street and into a park. There was a children's playground in the middle, a little wooden house and a sandpit covered in overgrown vines behind it.

He ran and hid himself quickly just as the boys emerged from the side road.

"Come out, come out, wherever you are," one of them sang in a falsetto.

Ben held his breath as the footsteps approached.

"He must be in there," one voice said.

The sound of a baseball bat thudding into wood broke the air as the boys attacked the little house.

"It's empty, you idiot," another voice said. "He must have run down the other way. Let's go. There's plenty more fun to be had today."

Their footsteps grew quieter. Ben let out his breath softly. He waited a few more minutes to be sure they were gone, then shook himself free from the sandpit. He pulled the vines off his arms, brushing his full-sleeve tattoos clean of the dirty sand.

Time to get out of here.

He headed out of the park and into a residential area. It was quiet; he supposed the residents had evacuated already. The place certainly felt abandoned. There were a couple of cars left on the street, deliberately parked as opposed to being dropped there by the gigantic wave. His father had taught him more than a few practical tricks, and it didn't take long to get one of them started.

He drove towards the city first, thoughts of Lucy and his father swirling in his mind. But at a fork in the road towards Christchurch, a pile of rubble dumped by the ocean blocked his way. He considered his options. There was only one that he could see: the road south was clear. The road towards Tekapo and Grandfather. The old man would know what to do and Ben still felt drawn there somehow.

He looked to the horizon, where a swirling mass of black clouds descended upon the land. The thick, inky blackness rolled across the sky. He thought he could see a misshapen face in the smoke, one with eyes of pitch and fangs of ash. A bolt of lightning shot through the black and the face dissipated.

Hurry, Ben.

His grandfather's voice. He had to go. His father would be fine and Lucy … Ben pushed aside his dark thoughts.

***

He drove southwest as night fell. The smoke mingled with the encroaching darkness, and the tiny bulbs in the car's headlights could not cut through it all. As Ben wove his way, he thought of the black smoke that had seemed to possess the gang. How long would it be before all-out anarchy gripped his beloved island?

A little further on, Lake Tekapo glowed like a plate of silver in front of him, the water rippled by an unseen wind. Ben scanned the horizon until he identified his grandfather's house ahead by the outline of the roof. The chimney still jutted from the top. That, at least, was a good sign.

His grandfather's home had always been a refuge, especially when his father's drunken violence had run on for days. He used to escape here and carve wood next to his grandfather before fishing on the lake together in the quiet of dusk.

But now it was too quiet. An eerie silence hung over the lake. Not even the insects made a sound.

The wind picked up, and on the gust came the odor of decaying flesh. The sky shifted, the clouds bleeding red. Shadows like claws crawled down from the hills. Ben shivered as an ominous feeling crept over him.

He drove quickly to his grandfather's house and parked outside. He got out of the car, slamming the door hard. The sharp noise echoed in the still air, but there was no other sound. Ben walked up the front steps towards the door, each foot putting pressure on the wooden stairs and cracking in the quiet.

The porch swing rocked back and forth in the breeze, creaking slightly. The chair where the old man spent countless evenings staring at the lake sat empty. Broken bottles lay strewn across the porch and his grandfather's fishing poles lay tangled in the corner as if tossed there by a giant.

Ben's hand shook as he reached for the doorknob. His fingers touched the cold brass. He slowly turned the knob until the door popped open a few centimeters. It was as dark inside as it was out. Then, he caught a whiff of tobacco from inside the house.

"Grandfather?" he called.

There was no reply.

Not a single sound. He pushed the door fully open as shadows lengthened around him.

"Grandfather? Are you here?"

BBC WORLD
NEWS REPORT:
BREAKING NEWS

THOUSANDS ARE REPORTED DEAD as a series of earthquakes rocked New Zealand this afternoon. At 3.11pm, the first earthquake occurred 4 km off the coast of Christchurch at a shallow depth. Measuring 7.3 on the Richter scale, it drove a tsunami towards the coast, devastating the coastal community. There was no warning of the quake.

This was followed by several more earthquakes near Te Anau and another at Dunedin, impacting much of the area south of Queenstown and Moeraki. Aftershocks have continued to rock the South Island, causing extensive damage to buildings and infrastructure. Pictures from smart phones and videos recorded locally show scenes of destruction and disturbing images of dead bodies, drowned or crushed by falling buildings. Communications are down and a state of emergency has been declared in the country. Australia is sending aid and medical staff to assist the New Zealand government at this difficult time.

The New Zealand Earthquake Commission (EQC) has advised people to stay in their homes and follow the guidelines of safety in earthquake areas.

Vulcanologist Michael Brown, currently situated in Sydney, Australia, issued a statement explaining the events.

"New Zealand is on the Pacific Rim of Fire, a geologically active zone with several thousand earthquakes a year. Most aren't even noticed but we have seen big quakes before so this is not entirely unusual. In 1931, 256 people died in Hawkes Bay and in 2011, 185 people lost their lives in the Christchurch quake. New Zealand has survived these disasters before and it will do so again."

CHAPTER 4

LUCY LOOKED AROUND. THE kitchen had somehow survived intact, braced by thick walls that held it up even as the rest of the house had fallen around it. The oak table was laid for their family dinner. Glasses lay on their sides, plates broken on the floor. There were pans in the sink, ready to be washed. It looked almost normal.

"Mum," Lucy called. "Dad … Amber."

A peal of bells began to ring outside, a warning from the local church. Sirens pierced the air, and there were screams in the distance.

But there was no sound in the house.

Lucy walked through the kitchen towards the sitting room where the Campion family would gather to watch films together. They all loved action movies, even Amber, who pretended she was too cool but would always sneak in as the credits rolled.

The room was the center of the house, where they would sit to watch the ocean beyond; where her parents would have their afternoon tea.

Something creaked and then thudded to the floor next door. Lucy started forward, running to the entrance of the sitting room.

It was a ruin.

Thick timber beams lay across the room, broken like straws. Dust rose from the one that had just fallen. Metal struts, exposed by the shearing of the house, poked out from a pile of bricks and dust and debris. The floor above had collapsed, opening the space to the sky. Storm clouds whirled high above.

Tears ran down Lucy's cheeks as she bent to pull a figurine from the rubble. A little ballerina. One of her mother's collection, born from a love of ballet that neither of her daughters had shared. For a moment, Lucy regretted the times she could have gone with her mother to the ballet. What if there would never be another chance?

She coughed. The air was thick with dust from the rubble pile, but she had to try and shift some of the debris.

Lucy pulled away the bigger pieces of fallen masonry first, leaning on her good leg, digging towards where her parents usually sat together on the sofa.

A cold certainty crept into her heart with every minute that passed, but she had to know for sure.

She dragged away the bricks, her hands bleeding with tiny cuts from the sharp plaster, nails snagging at her. She heaved away a final piece of timber, then stopped.

There they were.

Her mother lay crushed sideways, her neck bent at an unnatural angle by a heavy beam that had fallen from above. Her father's arms were wrapped around his wife, his body bent close to hers. His face was covered in dust. Tears of blood had run from his eyes and dried in the dirt. Even without medical training, Lucy would have known they were dead.

She fell to her knees in the rubble, letting grief pour from her in waves of tears. The whole city was broken, but her epicenter was here.

"Lucy … help." A thin, reedy call came from upstairs.

"Amber?"

Lucy got to her feet, wiping her eyes. Could her sister really be alive?

She climbed around the rubble and headed for the stairs. A few remained to the upper level, where half the house still stood. Lucy clambered up them.

"Amber! I'm coming," she called, pulling herself the last few feet and racing down what was left of the corridor to her sister's room.

Amber lay huddled under the bed, her blue eyes wide with fright.

"You came back." Amber's voice was soft.

Lucy lay down beside the bed. She took her sister's hands and rubbed her cold skin, suddenly aware of her own wet clothes and the ache in her bones, as well as her heart. Her leg still throbbed with pain.

There was another creak from downstairs, and a crunch as something else fell onto the rubble pile. Lucy knew there were aftershocks coming – possibly hundreds more, as there had been after the 2011 quake.

"We have to get out of here," she said quietly. "The house isn't safe. We need to get to central Christchurch and join the evacuation there."

Amber shook her head.

"No, Mum and Dad said we'd be fine here. They're downstairs. We'll wait here for everything to be normal again. It's fine."

Lucy couldn't help the tears that welled in her eyes.

"No," Amber whispered, shaking her head as realization dawned. "No. No. Please."

Lucy held out her arms and Amber scrambled out from under the bed into her embrace. The sisters wept together, Lucy rocking them gently in shared grief.

But the minutes ticked by, the earth continued turning, and Lucy knew they couldn't stay here and survive. The roads were ruined; no emergency vehicles would make it out this far. They had to get to the central area and meet up with the emergency services there. The country had planned for this type of disaster. They would be OK there.

"It's only us now," Lucy whispered. "And we need to go. Mum and Dad would have wanted us to be safe."

Amber nodded, sitting up and wiping her eyes.

"We can't take too much," Lucy said, "but can you find your backpack while I get some dry clothes?"

Amber stood and took a deep breath. "I've got some chocolate round here somewhere, too."

Lucy smiled. "I could use some of that."

She walked carefully into the next room, acutely aware of the house shifting beneath them. Her parents' bedroom was almost completely intact, but Lucy's room across the hallway had disappeared, crushed into the floor below. Lucy dug into her mother's chest of drawers, pulling out underwear, a pair of jeans, a t-shirt and a warm fleece. They were similar sizes, her mother retaining a trim figure by walking the peninsula every day. Lucy brought the fleece to her nose and inhaled the scent of her mother's perfume. Memories flooded back and she recalled the warmth of an embrace she would never feel again.

Tears pricked at Lucy's eyes, but she blinked them away. There would be time for grieving later. They needed to get out of here and into town before dark, before aftershocks pulled down the remaining shelter. The fresh water and electricity were down, the cabling and pipes ruptured, so they needed to get to the central area for help.

Lucy tugged off her wet clothing, wincing as she peeled away the trousers from her bad leg. She pulled on clean underwear, t-shirt and fleece, then she put her foot up on the bed and examined the wound. The bruising was deep purple and almost black in places, but the cuts weren't deep. She walked into her parents' en suite and grabbed the first aid pack from the bathroom cabinet. Lucy cleaned the wound, spraying it with antiseptic. She popped a couple of painkillers and hoped Amber would save her some chocolate as a sugar chaser.

She pulled on the jeans and grabbed her father's backpack from the cupboard. It was heavy, so she looked inside. It had a portable first aid kit, a small stove with a half-full gas canister, and some matches. There was also a Platypus water filter, something they had used on a recent camping trip. Her dad loved gadgets, and this was the latest tramping tech. You could put dirty water in the top part and it would filter through quickly and safely. No need for those disgusting iodine tablets, or even boiling. This would all come in handy if the emergency services were struggling.

Lucy grabbed a couple more pairs of underwear and t-shirts, plus two beanie hats and waterproofs for her and Amber, and stuffed them in the pack. She put on her mum's walking shoes and headed back to Amber's room. *Amazing what a change of clothes can do to make you feel human again*, Lucy thought.

The pitter-patter of rain came from the hallway, falling down from the hole in the house to the ruins beneath. The light dimmed as clouds gathered overhead.

Lucy pulled the waterproofs back out of the pack and put hers on over the fleece top. They couldn't stay here, especially if the weather was turning again. The house could shift under them, crushing even as it sheltered.

She thought of her parents downstairs.

No, not her parents anymore, but the bodies of what had once been the people she loved. Lucy knew that what had made them special was gone now. Their bodies could remain here in the cocoon of the broken house until the emergency services made it out here. They were not the only dead on this terrible day, Lucy knew that for sure.

But Christchurch had survived catastrophe before, and the emergency procedures were in place. They just had to get off the peninsula and further west inland, to where the bulk of the population were. Then they could join up with Civil Defense and they would be safe.

"Come on, Amber," Lucy called. "We need to get going."

Amber stepped from her room, her young face set with that Campion determination. Lucy smiled. She had seen that look on her dad's face when he was determined to solve a problem, no matter what.

The sisters clambered down the stairwell.

Amber paused in what had been the living room, looking at the huge pile of rubble.

"You have to go round the other side if you want to see them," Lucy said softly.

Amber shook her head. "I want to remember them how they were."

She reached out her hand and Lucy took it, squeezing a little.

"We've still got each other," she said.

A crash of lightning came from high above. A flash and then a roll of thunder. The rain began to fall more heavily, running down the rubble to pool at their feet in dirty grey puddles.

Lucy turned and headed into the kitchen. Amber followed. They grabbed some energy bars, fruit and cake from the cupboards and put them in the packs. Lucy thought it would only take them a couple of hours to reach the evacuation area, so they didn't need much.

Then they headed out into the darkening evening, faces set towards the northwest.

CHAPTER 5

"I'm through here." His grandfather's voice was rich and warm. Ben felt a wave of relief to hear it. "Come in and have some tea."

Ben walked inside, his eyes adjusting to the semi-darkness. At first it seemed like the house had somehow been spared the devastation of the quakes. There was the rimu table they had carved together back in the years when his mother was alive. There was the cloak of feathers hanging on the wall, the mark of a *kaumatua* – one of the elders of the tribe. The *taiaha* hung next to it, a Maori weapon of whalebone. Ben could smell his grandfather's homemade kawakawa tea under the tobacco, but it couldn't disguise the whiff of raw earth and natural gas. Something was leaking. They wouldn't be safe here for long.

As Ben's eyesight sharpened, he saw what the

quake had done. Picture frames lay in shattered pieces on the floor and cabinets hung askew on the far side of the kitchen. The television lay face down on the thin carpet, and his grandfather's potted plants had tumbled to the ground, where they rested in one corner.

His grandfather emerged from the tiny kitchen and navigated around the fallen bookcases. His face was marked with tribal *moko* tattoos, the black lines delineating ancient paths. The old man leaned in and pressed his nose and forehead to Ben's in the *hongi* greeting, the sharing of one breath. Ben felt the strength in the old man's arms, the wiry muscles honed by hiking in the mountains and chopping wood. His grandfather, Tamati, lived close to the land.

"The walls are cracked," Ben said as Tamati pulled away.

The old man nodded. "You should see the back-yard." He chuckled, a smile creasing his weathered face. "I'm so glad you made it. I thought perhaps…" His words trailed off. "Well, you're here now and I have much to tell you. But first, tea. It's cold, mind you. I didn't want to risk the stove."

Tamati poured out a cup and handed it over. Ben sipped it, the sharp taste welcome. He was parched. He gulped the rest down and Tamati refilled the cup.

"Were you at the boatyard when it happened?"

"No, Gramps. I was on the water with Lucy."

Ben felt ice grip his heart when he spoke her name. He hadn't ever explained their relationship to his grandfather but he figured the old man had worked it out.

"Is she –?"

"I don't know. The wave separated us."

Tamati nodded. "The gods are angry. But your girl …" He smiled. "She's a survivor. Now drink up. We need to get out of here and go further west."

"Because of the aftershocks?"

"Of course. But there is something far worse coming." Tamati raised an eyebrow. "You've seen it."

Ben was silent for a moment.

The tentacles in the wave. The smoke that whirled around the boys. It was more than an earthquake. More than a tidal wave.

He shook his head. "You know I don't believe in all that."

Tamati shrugged. "It doesn't matter what you believe. The time is here regardless, and they are coming again. After so long, they are rising."

"Demons? Monsters?" Ben asked.

"Gods. Risen Gods."

Ben raised an eyebrow at the words. Ever since he was a young child, he had listened to his grandfather's myths and fables. He had loved the stories back then, but they were just that – stories. Maori believed in many gods and creatures, some of which could destroy the world in an instant. But that seemed a long way from his practical urban life.

"It was only an earthquake," Ben insisted. "A tidal wave. Natural phenomena."

Tamati shook his head, his eyes darkening. "We've abused our home, Ben. Their home. And now they're coming to reclaim it. They will wash us away, rid the world of the human plague and return it to how it was in the Time Before."

Ben stood up, pacing with frustration. "This isn't some mythical beast attacking New Zealand. It was an earthquake, and the government will know what to do. They'll take control, restore order. It won't take long for the Red Cross to –"

Tamati held his hand up to stop Ben speaking. "Enough. I need to show you something."

Ben sat and waited as his grandfather walked down the hallway into the back bedroom. There was the sound of breaking glass, and then a long scraping noise. Tamati returned with a small box in his hands.

The black wood was shot through with a dark red grain, the finish as shiny as if his grandfather had just polished it. Ben caught the scent of silver beech and sandalwood.

Tamati handed the box to Ben. He took it reluctantly, then stiffened as a slight vibration surged through his fingers and up his arms. He used his forefinger to flick the brass latch open, but then hesitated before he lifted the lid.

"What is it?" he asked.

His grandfather clasped his hands to his chest.

"Open it," he said.

Ben took a deep breath and lifted the lid.

The box held an intricate bone carving with a leather string woven through a clasp. It portrayed a giant octopus with tentacles like the ones he had seen beneath the wave in the seconds before it pulverized the coast. Ben's stomach tightened and his head throbbed.

"It has been handed down through generations of *kaumatua*," Tamati said, his voice solemn. "A talisman to offer to the gods at a time of great struggle. Legend tells of a place in the ancient ice where the veil between the worlds grows thin. We must take it there, but I'm old, Ben." He sighed. "I need your help to go west."

Ben slammed the lid down, shaking his head. He put the box onto the table and stood.

"This is crazy. We should go back to Christchurch. Find Dad and Lucy."

Tamati put his hand on Ben's arm. He could feel his grandfather's strength even as the wrinkles on his face betrayed his age.

"You must take me, Ben. We don't have much time. We must get through the mountain pass to the glacier and find the ice cave. We can still save Aotearoa from the wrath of the Risen Gods."

"No." Ben strode towards the door. "I'm heading north again. And you're coming with me. Grab your things."

Ben stepped out into the darkness of the yard, his anger bubbling over. His grandfather had always been the wise one of the family. But this stuff was crazy. He would get the car started and they would head north again.

He took a step towards the car. Suddenly the darkness swirled about him. Black smoke thickened, and the stench of the dead filled the air.

Something was here.

"Ben!" Tamati stepped from the door of the house. He pulled the cloak of feathers about him, the bone *taiaha* staff in his hands. "We're too late. Get the talisman and go. You must get to the glacier."

The heavy black cloud swirled around Tamati and the reek of rotting flesh and sulfur filled the air. A face formed in the smoke – the same one Ben had seen in the clouds. Tendrils of blood-red morphed into claws as the thing curled around Tamati, raking at his cloak like a cat playing with its prey.

"Run, Ben. Go. This is my fate now. Yours lies ahead."

Tamati began to chant ancient words in *Te Reo*, the Maori language. His arms fluttered as he thrust at the smoke with the *taiaha*, eyes bulging as he stomped the ground in a challenge to the demonic force. It was as if he grew in stature, no longer an old man but a warrior facing his foe, desire for blood burning inside.

The face of the demon twisted at the challenge, and a roar bellowed from deep within the cloud. Ben fell to his knees as the sound shook the earth. The smoke tightened around Tamati, turning into sharp edges that struck at him, ripping at his flesh. As his grandfather's blood touched the earth, Ben ran forward.

"No!" He rushed into the smoke, arms outstretched to pull Tamati away.

He was thrust back by a mighty force, propelled back into the doorway of the house as the smoke turned into a whirlwind that surrounded his grandfather.

Ben saw the cloak of feathers stripped away, his grandfather's clothes slashed from him and then strips of his flesh torn off. Tamati howled his agony as the demon ripped at him. The light dimmed in Tamati's eyes and he threw his head back as his bones emerged from the flayed body.

Ben struggled to his feet, clutching at the doorpost at the horror of what he'd seen, unable to believe it was real.

But his grandfather's cries struck at his heart. He couldn't let his death be in vain.

He sprinted into the house and grabbed the box containing the talisman. He ducked back outside and darted around the spinning vortex of bloody smoke and chunks of flesh as the demon devoured what was left of Tamati.

Ben jumped into the 4WD and reversed out of the drive, his eyes fixed on the slaughter one last time. Tears streamed down his face, blurring his vision as he turned and sped off into the night, away from the horror and west through the mountains. He would take the talisman to the ice caves. He would honor his grandfather's wishes, no matter what it took.

CHAPTER 6

AN ALARM BLARED AS an aftershock rippled through the street. A crash of glass and shards shattered across the road, catching the light as they fell. Sitona stood on a street corner as mobs of people streamed by. An elderly woman stumbled as she passed and he caught her arm, helping her upright as the ground shook beneath them. She had a gash above her right eye and blood dripped from her cheek. Sitona took a bandana from his pocket and wiped the woman's face.

"Thank you," she said, her voice choked in a tired whisper.

Sitona smiled as she stumbled away towards a group of family members who called her name. Family was everything in times like these.

The apartment building on the opposite side of Montreal Street creaked and then collapsed. Sitona watched the top floors slide down to the east as plaster, glass and bricks tumbled to the street below. Clouds of dust filled the air, choking his lungs and making it hard to see. Two vehicles slammed into each other in the middle of the intersection in front of him. One driver burst through the windshield and flew over the other car, while the other driver became engulfed by the exploding airbag.

This is not like 2011, Sitona thought. *This is something else.*

He saw people dragging bodies out of the wreckage but he was frozen, unable to help. He fell to his knees.

Screams. Pain. Darkness.

He closed his eyes, and the sounds of Christchurch merged with those of Aceh years before, when the tsunami had gouged the Indonesian coast. He remembered the feel of the warm, greasy water and the smell of oil and human waste. The wave had silenced the screams back then. Sitona cursed the elements, and his fingers cramped up as they had during the many hours he had clutched a tree as the water raged beneath. He had survived the tsunami that dark day, but his fiancée had not. The gods of the ocean had yanked her from his grasp like another piece of flotsam.

I can't do this again, he thought. The screech of metal made him open his eyes. It was chaos.

He pushed himself backwards until he felt the external wall of the building behind. He pressed his hands back against it, taking a deep breath as he tried to anchor himself to the concrete structure. But then he realized that if this building came down next, he'd be forever buried beneath it.

Sitona forced himself up, and walked away from the shadow of the building. He fished the satellite phone from his pocket and tapped in his cousin's number. Sitona had always thought the phone was an extravagant expense, and that the Indonesian government wasn't as corrupt as Juno claimed it to be. Now, amidst the ruin and devastation of Christchurch, he was grateful to have a wireless phone that worked.

"Sito. Are you OK?"

Sitona exhaled as he heard his cousin's voice. He couldn't speak for a moment.

"Sito. Is that you?"

"Yeah, Juno. It's me. I'm fine."

"Holy shit, bro. What the hell is happening there?"

"Earthquake and a lotta water. Not as bad as Aceh but things here are screwed."

A woman screamed for help as she ran past. She carried a lifeless child in her arms, the corpse covered in grey dust and blood.

"People are dying," said Sitona.

"Yeah, no shit. You in a safe place?"

"Not yet."

"Hang up and go find yourself a safe spot. A refuge. Call me back when you've done that. Keep it together now. For the family."

Sitona nodded.

"OK. I'll call you later."

Sitona ended the call. Juno was right. He had to pull himself together and find shelter.

He ran to the corner of Montreal Street and Hereford and looked up at the Christchurch City Council Water and Waste Unit. The six-story concrete building seemed unaffected by the disaster. It stood upright with a few shattered windows, but it appeared structurally intact.

He ran up to the main doors and yanked. They were locked. He turned and picked up a garbage can from the sidewalk and threw it into the glass doors.

They shattered.

Sitona waited, but nobody came to investigate or try to prevent him from entering. The building probably had thousands of square feet of space, and yet he saw nobody. Sitona stepped inside as another aftershock rumbled beneath his feet. He put both hands out and steadied his balance as it passed. It was minor, but it still triggered another round of screaming alarms.

As Sitona climbed into the building, a flash of movement caught his eye. He turned and saw a young boy standing alone on the sidewalk. A trickle of blood ran down the side of his face and his dark brown eyes were wide. The boy's hair was white with brick dust, and his t-shirt hung in shreds from his thin body.

"Come with me," Sitona said quietly so as not to alarm him. "I'm going somewhere safe."

The boy stood unblinking. He didn't move, but he didn't run either.

"You're in shock," Sitona said, his arms outstretched towards the boy. "I'm an adult. You can trust me. C'mon. I'll get us somewhere safe and then we'll call for help. I've got one of these, too." He pulled out the phone. "It will work 'cause it's a satellite. Earthquakes can't hurt things in space, right?"

The boy gave a slight smile, and his shoulders dropped a bit.

A building across the street exploded, raining glass down upon Hereford Street. Flames caught high above and screams came from the building. The ground rumbled beneath their feet. A man fell from the upper floor, his body crunching to the sidewalk below.

The boy dove into Sitona's arms. Sitona turned

and carried the child through the doors of the Water and Waste Unit. They would be safe here, at least for a while.

Light came from the windows on the external walls, but it couldn't reach any deeper into the building. They walked on into the gloom until they reached steps leading down to a basement. Sitona stared down into the gaping, black mouth of the stairwell. A soft, rancid pulse of air moved across his face, carrying with it the smell of rotting things and leaking pipes. There were tendrils of black smoke hanging in the air like a mist.

"I don't want to go down there," the boy whispered.

"Neither do I," Sitona said, ruffling the boy's hair. "If this floor collapses we'll die down there. Let's go this way instead."

Sitona led the way deeper into the building, down a corridor where a single shaft of thin light fell on the dull grey industrial carpet. At the first open door he turned into a cramped office, the boy by his side. Empty shelves hung on the wall, but the three-ring binders that had been stacked on them lay on the ground like birds with broken wings. There was a half-full water cooler and a stack of single-serve cereal boxes beneath it.

"Someone must have liked eating at their desk," Sitona said, waving the child inside. He noticed a set of keys dangling from the knob, the one for the room still in the lock. There were no windows.

"Get yourself some cereal and a drink of water. You'll be safe here."

The boy scooted inside, grabbing a box of Coco Pops. Sitona smiled and yanked the keys from the knob. He shoved them in his pocket while the boy stuffed handfuls of dry cereal into his mouth.

"What's your name?" Sitona asked.

"Josh," the boy said between mouthfuls.

"How old are you, Josh?"

"Nine."

"Good, good," Sitona said. "What happened to your parents?"

"The building came down. They couldn't get out."

"So they died?"

The boy nodded. He stopped eating and looked at Sitona through a veil of tears.

"I'm sorry to hear that. Do you have any brothers or sisters?"

"No."

"Any other relatives in Christchurch?"

"No."

Josh stood and took a step towards the door. Sitona stepped sideways and blocked his exit from the room.

"I'm gonna take care of you now. I'll keep you

safe. First thing I gotta do is lock the door and keep the bad people from getting inside."

"With you?" Josh asked.

"No. I have to stay at the main door and make sure they don't get in that way. I'm going to lock you in to protect you, alright?"

Josh's eyes darted around the room, looking for escape. Sitona took a step towards the door and grabbed the handle.

"Just go to sleep," he said. "I'll be back for you."

Josh ran towards him, but Sitona was too fast.

He stepped out of the room and pulled the door shut, locking it. The boy pounded on the other side and cried out.

"Let me out!"

Sitona slid the keys into his pocket and walked to the front of the building. He took out his phone, then hesitated for a moment. His heart pounded, but he was committed now.

He looked out into the darkness and blocked out the boy's screams. Business was business, and the kid would probably be dead without him.

He dialed his cousin's number again,

"Things are good now, and I have an idea. Market's gonna be flooded with product. Then it'll go dry once the government rolls in with disaster relief."

"Cocaine? Meth?"

"Nah, Juno. You can only sell that shit once. I'm talking product we can sell again and again."

"Bitches?" Juno asked.

"Think bigger. The whores always run away. I'm going with a safer play."

"Oh, shit, Sito. I like how you're thinking. We can get top dollar for kids."

"That's right. And I already got one in the stable. Lots of dead parents, which means –"

"Lots of orphans."

"Yep. We're gonna be rich. I'm heading out to see what else I can find. Must be a ton of kids looking for somewhere to hide out."

CHAPTER 7

THE SCENES OF DESTRUCTION only seemed to worsen as Lucy and Amber walked into Christchurch city center. The full force of the wave had crashed down here, mashing buildings to dust, crushing those within back to the earth. The encroaching night was a blessing as it limited their vision of what the city had lost. They had rebuilt once before, but as Lucy looked around, she couldn't see how Christchurch would rise again from this.

There was a tension in the air, as if the collective energy of a suffering people had risen into a cloud that hung over the city. The aftershocks kept coming sporadically, pulsing through the earth.

A scream pierced the air. Not of grief this time, but fear. At times like this, people lost the thin veneer of civility that enabled a society to function. There was a flashlight in her backpack, but Lucy thought it was safer to walk in the darkness. They didn't want to draw attention to themselves.

The sisters held hands, and Lucy felt Amber's grip tighten every time they heard a wail from the darkness. They walked in the middle of the road, away from the buildings, skirting around the rippled tarmac that broke apart the streets. Any houses that were still standing teetered on broken spars, lumps of concrete crashing to the ground as the aftershocks came in waves.

Amber kept her eyes fixed forward, looking neither right nor left, concentrating on getting to the evacuation station. Lucy could only hope that the trauma wouldn't leave her sister in deep shock. She was sure that Civil Defense and perhaps even the military would have everything in order soon, but she would need her little sister to function in the coming hours.

A couple limped across the road in front of them, the man holding the woman around the waist as she hobbled on what looked like a broken leg. The woman's face was bloody, her eyes hollow as she leaned on him for support. Lucy recognized the woman, Mrs Bennett, a history teacher she had once known at high school not far from here. She remembered the prim pencil skirts, the buttoned-up blouse, the woman's perfect hairstyle. Now,

Mrs Bennett's long black hair was matted, her torn clothes covered in dust.

Lucy opened her mouth to speak, but then hesitated. *What was even left to say on this terrible night?* she thought. She slowed down, holding Amber back to let the couple pass in front of them on the road, heading for the darkness of the houses beyond.

As they crossed, there was a sudden hiss of leaking gas. The ground split as a fissure opened up in the road directly in front of the couple.

A plume of hot steam rushed upwards.

The pair screamed as they were caught in the middle of the flow. The man instinctively propelled himself forward, but Mrs Bennett tripped and dropped to the ground. She writhed as boiling steam surrounded her and agonized screams wracked the air.

The man turned back.

"Miriam," he shouted. His voice cracked as he tried to reach her but was driven back by the intensity of the heat. The woman curled on the ground and was still. The man turned in desperation to Lucy and Amber. "Please, help me."

Lucy had seen thermal burns from steam. Mrs Bennett was as good as dead because there was no way to treat her here, no way to get her to a burns unit which would be swamped anyway. The doctor part of her wanted to stay and help, but she also understood the nature of triage. There was nothing they could do. Lucy tugged on Amber's hand, pulling her away quickly to the side of the road, skirting the dreadful scene and walking quickly onwards towards the city center.

As they walked away, Lucy's mind whirled. Guilt tore through her. She couldn't have saved her parents, but she could have helped Mrs Bennett. The oath of a doctor was to preserve life, to do no harm. They should have stopped.

What if it had been her and Amber trapped in the steam? Would the couple have helped? Would they have risked their lives for strangers?

Lucy shook her head, willing the images of the dying woman away. But she wouldn't turn from helping again; she would join the medics with Civil Defense. She just had to get Amber somewhere safe first.

The roads became busier as the sisters finally made it into the central area of Christchurch. Streams of people walked alongside, some in groups, others striding alone. Most were silent, while others wept quietly. Parents clutched the hands of their children; others helped the elderly. On a street corner near the Avon River, a man rang a hand bell, its sonorous notes echoing through the streets, a lament for the crippled city. The crowd walked onwards towards Cathedral Square, the spiritual heart of Christchurch.

The cathedral had been ruined by the 2011 earthquake, the toppled spire a symbol of the crushed city. An innovative cardboard replacement had been used in the last few years. That was the focus of the crowd now. As they reached the center, Lucy looked up and around, noting that there was less damage here. Rebuilding in the central area had focused on earthquake-proof buildings, so it made sense that they would be more secure. A sense of hope kindled inside her at the potential safe haven that surrounded them. As the night progressed, they would need shelter soon enough.

They turned a corner into Cathedral Square. Bright lights attached to generators illuminated the area and people in fluorescent yellow jackets used megaphones to direct the masses.

"Keep walking, folks," a Maori woman called, her voice tired. "There's hot tea round the corner by registration."

A queue formed in front of the tea station and Lucy and Amber got in line. Around them, people whispered of what they had lost, but even in the depths of tragedy, people were behaving normally here. Lucy gave Amber a hug as they stood in line, stepping forward slowly to wait their turn.

"We're going to be OK," Lucy said. "We'll have our tea, then we'll register and soon, we'll be evacuated out of here. The rest of New Zealand helped last time. They will again."

A man in a yellow hazard jacket walked down the line.

"If there are any medics here, we could sure use the help," he called into his megaphone.

Without thinking, Lucy found her hand going up.

"I'm a medical student," she said as the man strode over.

Amber pulled on her arm.

"Don't leave me," she whispered.

But Lucy couldn't get the dying woman from her mind.

"We're OK now. I'll come find you as soon as I've helped out. You know that's what Mum and Dad would have wanted."

The man pointed out a Red Cross tent on the far side of the square.

"The medical staff are over there." He leaned closer so the people around them wouldn't over-hear. "They need urgent help with the injured who made it this far. There are other roving teams." He frowned. "But they're only bringing back bodies at the moment. We're swamped."

"Aren't we getting help from Dunedin or other cities?" Lucy asked.

The man shook his head. "You haven't heard, then. The whole South Island has been rocked by earthquakes. There's even word of trouble brewing in the North. For now, the city has to look after itself."

"I'll go help right now," Lucy said, even as her mind reeled at the implications of his words.

The man carried on down the line, calling for medics and nurses and anyone who could help practically with the crisis.

"Please don't leave me," Amber whispered again. Lucy grasped her shoulders and faced her.

"We're Campions," she said, her voice strong. "Our family has been in this country for generations. This land is part of our blood. These people are our people. We have to help."

Amber took a deep breath and then nodded.

"How will I find you again later?"

Lucy looked at the queue for the tea and then on to registration. It all looked orderly and well run. In the aftermath of crisis, the volunteers were making sure people were alright.

"Stay in line and follow the directions of the volunteers. They'll have tents for you to sleep in, and hot food. I'll find you later." Amber's eyes were full of doubt. Lucy smiled at her. "I promise you. I won't leave you. Look how organized this is. I'll come find you later."

Lucy gave her sister a hug and then crossed the square, heading for the Red Cross tent. As she reached the centerpoint, she looked back at the long line of people. She waved at Amber, smiling encouragement.

As her sister waved back, the earth heaved.

Lucy was thrown to the ground as a massive after-shock sent a wave of energy through the square. A roar of destruction filled her ears. A rumble came from below the earth and then the ground rent apart.

Screams split the air.

A huge office block toppled down, crashing into the square, cutting off Lucy's view of where Amber had stood only moments before.

CHAPTER 8

AS DAWN BROKE, BEN drove out of the mountain pass and headed north towards the Franz Josef glacier. The night had been long, his mind filled with images of his grandfather's end, the grisly scene replaying over and over. He still didn't understand what the hell was going on, but he had to accept that this was more than a natural disaster now. Whatever the truth, he would take the talisman to the ice. The question was, where was the cave?

Ben pulled over and took the talisman from its box. He tied it round his neck, tucking it inside his shirt so it lay against his skin. It pulsed there like a living thing. A strange sensation, but it didn't feel like the black smoke. Perhaps it would show him where it belonged. Ben shook his head at the thought. Not so long ago, he had dismissed the myths. Look at him now.

He drove on and soon reached the small town servicing tourist trips to the glacier. Cars were parked at the edge of town and people milled around in groups. There was a military vehicle on one side of the road and a Red Cross truck on the other. People had lined up in front of both trucks to collect canned rations and bottled water. He definitely needed provisions before heading on, so Ben pulled over.

The place was familiar. He had been up here six months ago on a stag weekend for one of his cousins. Just a bit of fun with the boys. This little town sure knew how to party, even if there only was one decent bar.

He had met a girl that night, too.

Gina had been working at the bar, a young American with purple highlights in short blonde hair that framed her elfin features. Her hazel eyes had sparkled as they'd talked that night, and he had definitely tried to impress her with stories of his Kiwi adventures. After his cousin had been carried back to their hotel singing rugby songs, Ben had stayed behind and waited until the end of her shift. He'd walked Gina home, the night air cool around them as they held hands in the dark. He remembered kissing her under the stars, his head spinning a little. She smelled of coconut shampoo and tasted of butter toffee. He couldn't get enough of her.

But at the door to her place, she'd pressed a hand to his chest and leaned close. "I don't put out on the first date," she'd whispered. "But come back sometime, Ben."

Of course, he hadn't been back and he didn't even have her number. He had thought about Gina since, but then Lucy had returned from Uni on holidays and he'd consigned that night to memory. Now, he wondered if Gina was still here or if she'd moved on like so many backpackers working transient jobs to fund their overseas trip.

Ben opened the door of the truck and stepped out, walking to the back of a line that stretched towards the emergency distribution points. Beyond them, the huge face of the ancient glacier stretched into the distance. Franz Josef held enough mystery and danger to attract even the most adventurous visitors to New Zealand.

A cool wind blew off the ice and Ben shivered. He felt shaky, almost feverish. He hadn't really stopped since the wave and the shock of the demon and his grandfather's death were overwhelming. The queue moved forward and he stumbled a little into the man in front of him.

"Are you alright?" the man said as he turned around.

"Yes, sorry. Just … worried." Ben waved his arms around at the crowd, shaking his head.

The man nodded, his eyes darkening. "Everyone's heading north now. Trying to get over to Wellington, away from all this."

They talked a little as the line moved forward, swapping news of Christchurch and Dunedin. Suddenly, Ben found himself at the front as the man moved away from the line. He stared straight into the eyes of the young woman who served the queue.

Gina.

She looked up, holding out a ration pack.

"Oh," she said, her hand frozen in mid-air. "It's you."

Her purple highlights were tied back with a red headband and her multiple ear piercings sparkled in the sun. She wore a grey t-shirt with the glacier on it and tight black jeans hugged her slim figure. Her nails were short and chewed down, but her arms were toned from hard work. The West Coast wasn't for the weak.

"Hi." Ben reached for the rations, feeling like an idiot. "I meant to –"

Their fingers touched as he took the packet and he felt a jolt of attraction. It hadn't only been the beer that night.

Gina laughed, shaking her head. "I said come back, but you could have chosen a better time for it."

Ben grinned. It was like they'd seen each other yesterday.

"Let me finish handing this lot out," Gina said. "Then I'll come say hi."

Ben pointed over to where his truck was parked. "I'll wait over there," he said.

* * *

Gina watched Ben walk away, his steps slow and heavy across the parking lot. Something had happened to the happy young man she'd met a few months back – something more than the tidal wave and natural disaster. His physique was still as muscled and taut as she remembered, the full-sleeve tattoos of Maori design covering his arms. She remembered tracing the whorls, and how his skin had felt against hers that night. But his handsome face was shadowed now, dark circles beneath haunted eyes.

She had wanted to ask him in that night, but the tales he had told combined with his passion for the ocean had made her want more than just a fling. She had considered going after him, seeking him out at the boatyard he'd told her about in Christchurch. But she'd ended up staying for the season, making friends out here, and the days had passed along with her infatuation. The West Coast felt like the edge of civilization and she had come here to escape, not entangle herself again. New Zealand was a long way from Chicago and it was time to break the pattern.

Now Ben was back, even though the world was going to hell. She had planned to leave later that night, to head north in the evacuation with the gang from the bar. If he had come tomorrow, she would have gone. But now …

Gina turned back to the queue of people, handing out the ration packs more quickly now, eager for her shift to end.

* * *

Returning to the truck, Ben climbed in and closed his eyes. He leaned his head back on the rest and exhaled. Images of his grandfather's death whirled before him, visions of the destruction of Christchurch, of what he'd seen within the wave.

He didn't even know whether Lucy was alive, and here he was, thinking about another woman. But Gina's friendly face seemed like a lifeline and Ben clung to it. He would go on his way after catching up with her.

A sharp rap on the driver's side window made him jump and he opened his eyes. Gina stood on the other side, a backpack over one shoulder. Ben leaned over and pushed the door open. She climbed inside, turning sideways to look at him, her hazel eyes curious.

"What brings you back here?" She smiled softly. "Of course I'm pleased to see you, but this isn't exactly the direct route north from Christchurch."

Ben reached for her hand. "I meant to come back, you know. That night, it was –"

"I know," Gina said, her eyes meeting his. "It wasn't the right time. So, what are you doing here?"

Ben wanted to tell her about the wave, his grandfather, the demon in the smoke, but he knew it would sound crazy.

"I need to get up to the glacier," he said, looking pointedly at the military truck ahead of them.

"What's so important that you want to get up there now?" Gina asked. "They're evacuating to Greymouth, so it would be better to stick around for that, I reckon."

"I have to…" Ben's voice trailed off.

Have to what, exactly? Save the world from demons with a magical Maori talisman?

"What?" Gina asked. "What do you have to do?"

"My brother," Ben said, grasping for something rational to say. "He was climbing on the glacier. I haven't heard from him since the quakes hit."

"I'm so sorry," Gina's hazel eyes showed concern. "I didn't know you had a brother. But the soldiers said that no one can enter the park now. The quake may have opened fissures in the glacier. It's not safe."

Ben nodded, but he still looked towards the park entrance. "It might be best if I stayed here and waited for the authorities to give the all-clear."

"You're going anyway, aren't you?" Gina looked at him, her head cocked to one side. "Think maybe you need some company?"

The twitch at the side of her mouth and the sparkle in her eyes held a promise.

But Ben remembered the creature in the smoke, the way it had ripped his grandfather's flesh from his body. It wasn't safe to take anyone with him.

And Lucy. She had to be alive. He could feel it in some inexplicable way. *I have to find Lucy, and here I am flirting with this girl.*

"No," he said, shaking his head. "You stay here. You'll be safer getting evacuated."

"I want to help," Gina said. "I mean, this is your brother, right? And you can't go into the glacier alone. I've done a lot of ice climbing since you were here last. I've got some gear in there and I know the ice." She indicated the pack. "Face it, you need me."

Ben looked out at the glacier rising above the trees over the town. She was right – he didn't know the ice. If he died up there falling into a crevasse, his grandfather's dying request could not be honored. And if he were honest, it would be good to have some company – someone to keep his mind from the horror of the last days. Surely he had left the demon behind in Tekapo.

"If you're certain," he said.

Gina nodded. "I want to help. Do you know where your brother was last seen?"

Ben felt a tug from the talisman, like it drew him on. Like it was being called home.

"Not quite, but I'll know when we get there. We'll drive to the edge of the glacier, park up and then hike in."

They drove out of the area and down a side road, heading towards the glacier. As they approached, Ben looked out his window at the forbidding expanse of ice.

"You sure about this?" Gina asked.

"I have to find my brother," Ben said.

"What's his name?"

"Jerry," said Ben. It was the first name that came to mind.

"Ben and Jerry?" Gina raised her eyebrows and stifled a giggle.

They drove further and reached the trailhead, only to find soldiers at the entrance. The uniformed men walked the parking lot, tending to the injured and lost. Bright orange hazard cones stood in front of the trailhead, but no one was actively guarding the route. Ben guessed that they assumed no one would be crazy enough to head for the glacier at night, especially mere hours after a major earthquake.

"We're going to have to sneak past the men with guns to get in there," Gina said.

"Something you Americans are used to," Ben replied with a wide grin.

Gina tucked a strand of purple hair behind her ear. "We're not all riding around in Chevys with gun racks, asshole."

Ben backed up the truck and they parked a little way from the main lot so they were hidden in the trees. They filled their packs and checked their gear.

"It's getting dark. We'll head that way." Gina pointed towards the edge of the bush. "We can sneak round the main entrance and meet the path further down."

They dodged the emergency lights and ran alongside a wooden fence before heading down the trail into the gloom. They walked single-file down the track, maintaining a fast pace until the sounds of people behind them had faded.

Only their footsteps could be heard in the night air. A freezing wind blew from the glacier and the talisman burned against Ben's chest. It drew him deeper, towards the ice.

They continued in silence for the better part of an hour, until the trail came to a fork with a signpost. The darkness was close now, almost absolute. Ben couldn't read the sign, but Gina was confident even in the dark.

"Left takes us on a loop around the face of the glacier towards the main climbing area," she said. "Right takes us to the ice caves and it's unlikely your brother would be there. So it must be this way."

She turned left. Ben grabbed her elbow.

"Wait," he said.

From the deep ice, a steady, slow *drip drip* echoed like a gigantic clock.

"We need to go right," he said. "Into the caves. I'm sorry, but I haven't been honest with you. You need to make a choice, Gina."

CHAPTER 9

DUST FILLED THE AIR from the fallen building, and Lucy coughed as she tried to stand on the shaky ground. Above her, the night sky darkened and rain poured down from the heavens, the sound of lightning and thunder adding to the chaos. It was as if nature wanted to wipe the city from the earth and Lucy had a momentary sense of how small she was in the face of all this.

As the ground shuddered still, she got up and ran towards the massive concrete structure that now bisected the square.

"Amber!" she called, even as she knew there was no way her sister would hear her over the chaos. She beat her fists against the concrete, tears welling. She began to climb the rubble, the Red Cross tent forgotten in the need to be reunited with her sister.

* * *

As the building came down and then the shock rippled beneath her, Amber instinctively darted for the doorframe of a shop, throwing herself into it as the wave of energy pulsed beneath. She hit her head as she fell, but as the concrete crumbled around her, she managed to drag herself under the thickest part of the door.

The line she had stood in moments before was buried now, crushed beneath the huge tower.

Lucy was under there, she knew it.

Her sister was dead, just like their parents.

Amber wanted to curl up and close her eyes – to stay here and sleep and never see anything again. Her mind froze. She was alone. She had no one.

As the shocks calmed a little, the sounds of screams and crying filled the air. Volunteers rushed to help, but as they pulled bodies from the rubble, Amber knew this wasn't the end of the anguish.

There would be more shocks. There would be more death. There would be no help. She had heard the words of the man earlier: the entire country was in trouble.

Amber knew she had to get away from here. She couldn't stand the sound of grief and pain and terror any longer. They only stoked her own feelings of despair. There must be strong buildings near here where she could shelter for the night. She thought of the museum at Hagley Park. It was only a few blocks west. It was also somewhere that the Campion family used to visit regularly. Maybe Lucy was safe; maybe she would come and search there.

Amber pulled herself upright and leaned against the doorframe. She looked out over the ruins of the square, then turned away and hobbled south and west along Hereford Street.

As she crossed the river, a voice called from the shadows at the side of the bridge.

"Careful, child," a woman said. "The gods are angry and Aotearoa must pay the price in blood." She stepped from the shadows, her brown face marked with the Maori *moko* for women, blue-black ink on her lips and geometric patterns on her chin. "Be sure that yours is not among those called to sacrifice."

Amber shrank away from the fierce woman, hurrying on as the woman's laughter echoed behind.

As she passed the Christchurch City Council Water and Waste Unit down the road, she saw torchlight and the outline of a young man. He was smoking, the red end of his cigarette glowing bright.

"There's food here," he called out in a friendly tone. Amber was hungry, and her stomach rumbled at his words. The man looked Indonesian, with black hair like the friendly people she had met on holiday in Bali with her parents a few years back.

"You can shelter here," the man said. "There are some other kids too. Kids who have lost their families."

Amber was tired and hungry and desperate to rest. She had lost her family; maybe she should stop here with the other kids. Everything would be better in the morning – that's what Lucy always said. In the morning, the sun would shine. She would find her sister … She needed to eat right now, and get some sleep. Just for a little while.

She stepped towards the light.

***

The girl was slight and blonde. Pretty little thing. Must be about fourteen.

Perfect.

Sitona smiled as he waved her over, stubbing out his cigarette.

"You'll be safe here," he said. "We have some food, too."

"Are you sure it's safe?" the girl asked.

"Of course. If you come inside, you can meet the other kids and get some sleep."

"Is it dark inside?" The girl's voice shook a little.

"Yeah, kinda. But we got torches. What's your name?"

"Amber," she said.

"Follow me, Amber."

Sitona flashed her a jackal's grin and led Amber deeper into the building, where the shadows and darkness merged. He fished the keys from his pocket and unlocked the door. He pushed it open and several young, frightened faces looked up at them.

"What –"

Sitona shoved Amber into the room, cutting off her words, and slammed the door shut. She screamed and pounded on the other side. The noise echoed down the corridor as Sitona walked away. No one would come for her, and once they all drank the water he'd laced, they'd all be out cold and no trouble at all.

Now he needed to ship the product, and he knew just the place. Time to call in a favor.

He jogged down a few blocks to a rental place he knew that was gang-affiliated. A bearded man holding a shotgun sat at the front door. The man recognized Sitona and smiled, but kept the shotgun in his embrace.

"'Sup Sito?"

"You got vans?"

The man raised his eyebrows but didn't respond.

"Do you?"

"Those vans are worth a lot of money right now."

"Juno's coming down from Indo."

The bearded man paled a little and then nodded. He set the shotgun on the table and opened the door to the yard. Several vans had fallen into a gaping crevasse opened by the quake, but two remained in their normal parking spaces.

"You'll tell Juno I did you a solid, right? You'll tell him."

"Yeah, man. You got my word. But I need this van now."

The bearded man tossed Sitona a set of keys and stepped aside. "Take the one with the scorpion badge on the back. Better on the roads."

Sitona walked to the van, opened the door, and was immediately hit with the stink of dried coffee and stale beer. He climbed in, checked the cargo hold, and nodded. It was big enough for all of them. Now he had to get the product north.

CHAPTER 10

BY THE TIME LUCY made it over the rubble, the medics on the far side were pulling bodies from under the fallen building. They lay them in lines for identification and removal. It was a grisly sight.

"Amber!" Lucy called as she clambered down the other side, slip-sliding over the broken masonry. Her hands were bleeding, nails ripped. She was covered in dust and sweat and blood. Nothing mattered but Amber now. She couldn't lose her sister too.

Her calls were drowned by the cacophony of disaster. Lucy looked around in desperation, but she couldn't see Amber anywhere. She caught sight of the woman who had been behind them in the queue, sitting dazed on the ground, her eyes glassy and unseeing.

"Have you seen my sister?" Lucy asked, bending

down to kneel next to the woman. "She was near you earlier, before the building came down."

The woman stared at her, brown eyes suddenly focused.

"It's all lost," she whispered, shaking her head. "It's all gone this time."

Lucy turned away from the woman's grief, scanning the area around. But there was no sign of Amber.

Then she noticed where they were, right on the corner of the square with the road to the museum heading west. She and Amber had spent many days there over the years. If Amber had survived, if her body wasn't buried under the mounds of rubble, then perhaps she had gone to the museum.

Lucy's heart lifted with hope. Amber was alive – she wouldn't consider any other possibility.

She headed west.

At the bridge over the river, a Maori woman emerged from the darkness of the trees.

"Kia ora," she said. Lucy stopped at the greeting.

"I know you, girl." The woman's voice was rough. "I've seen you with Ben Henare. He's *motuhake* – special. He will need you in the final battle to come."

"Is Ben alive?" Lucy said. "You've seen him?"

"In a way, girl, I have." The Maori woman walked to the side of the bridge and stared down at the water. "I've seen him in the water and the trees and the birds, like I see all of us."

Lucy began to walk on. The woman was clearly crazy.

"And I've seen your sister, too."

Lucy spun around and jogged back.

"Where is she? Where's Amber?"

The woman shook her head.

"Bad men come at times of trouble. Bad things happen even to those who are on the side of the gods. Your sister has been taken. You must go to her, to Kaikoura and then onwards."

Lucy wanted to shake the woman.

"What do you mean she's been taken? Please. You have to know more."

The woman leaned forward, thrusting a hand out. A greenstone pendant dangled from it.

"Take this north. The *pounamu* will protect you on your journey. I can't do any more than that. My place is here, to witness the end, but you still have a chance, girl. Go now, before dawn flushes the sky. There is more destruction coming here. The gods are not finished with us yet."

The woman turned and walked away into the shadows, disappearing quickly into the darkness.

Lucy stood for a moment, unsure of what had just happened, unsure of what to do next. Should she trust the word of a crazy woman? She clutched the *pounamu* and then opened her hand, looking at the greenstone more closely.

It was a *manaia* design, representing a mythical creature with the head of a bird and the body of a man. To the Maori, the *manaia* was the messenger between the physical world and the domain of the spirits, used as a guardian against evil.

In the depths of her fear and grief, in the maelstrom of the Christchurch disaster, Lucy felt a calmness descend upon her. Perhaps she should go north. She loved Kaikoura, and the Campions had camped there for many summers. Ben had told her Maori myths of the place. It resonated with the spiritual power of the ocean, even to a Pakeha like her. She thought of Ben's laugh, the warmth of his hand in hers. They had fooled around as teens, but nothing serious. Both had dated other people, but now Lucy realized that it had always been him. The Maori woman seemed to suggest that their futures would somehow entwine; that the land itself was connected to their journey.

Lucy didn't know what to do. The darkness shrouded closer around her. The sound of running footsteps and sirens broke the night.

She couldn't stay here.

She would have to trust the woman. Kaikoura

was only a few hours north. She just needed a way to get there. She fastened the pendant around her neck and began to walk, heading for the road north. There would surely be trucks ferrying people towards Picton, towards Wellington, the capital on the southern tip of the North Island.

Exhaustion overwhelmed her, but Lucy didn't stop. She couldn't. Not now. If she stopped to rest, she wouldn't be able to get back up again. *One step after the next*, Lucy thought. *One more corner. Perhaps Amber will be there.*

She turned her face north and felt the wind from the ocean, smelled the sea on the air. It was a scent she associated with happiness, with exhilaration. She half smiled. Even after the destruction, it still meant that to her. It meant Ben. Could she trust that he was still alive?

"Quit sitting around, Henare," she whispered, sending her thoughts on the breeze, wishing them to him. "Meet me on the road to the north."

Her thoughts made the time pass quickly, and soon Lucy reached the highway. She thrust out her thumb as vehicles passed, headlights shining on the road ahead. Several rumbled past, faces peering out the side as they continued without stopping, packed full of fearful people.

Eventually, a Red Cross truck pulled over.

"We've space for you in here," the female driver called out.

Lucy ran over and pulled the door open. There were already four others squashed into the front seat, and the back of the truck was packed. The tang of sweat and the stink of blood and pus pervaded the air within. It was the smell of sickness. The smell of the near-dead. She got in.

"Thanks so much," Lucy said as the woman pulled into the traffic again.

"We're not leaving anyone behind," the driver said with gritted teeth. "We've lost enough tonight."

The truck was eerily silent, and the rocking movement soon sent Lucy into an exhausted sleep.

***

She woke as the fingers of dawn broke across the horizon. Lucy looked out the window to see the magnificence of the ocean before her. It was calm and flat. No one could have guessed the destruction it had wrought in the last twenty-four hours. The little town of Kaikoura lay ahead on the peninsula, but Lucy only had eyes for the sea.

This was one of the few places in the world where the deep waters were close to the shore. The upwelling from the Hikurangi Trench brought an abundance of marine life to feed here. Kaikoura came from the Maori words for 'meal of crayfish,' and it was here that people came to swim with dolphins and whales in the ocean, overlooked by the stunning Seaward Kaikoura mountains. The sun sparkled on the water, and Lucy longed to be out there.

The trials of real life slipped away when she was on the ocean and she sank into that sweet memory now. She remembered swimming from a boat out there, clad in a thick wetsuit with a weight belt to help her sink under. The cold permeated through it, chilling her skin. There'd been a moment when she had realized she floated above 3000 meters of water, her tiny body just a speck in the blue. She had looked down through the water with her dive mask and calmed her heartbeat. The blue stretched down in shades to black as she breathed deeply through the snorkel. There were whales here, dolphins … and sharks.

Then, Lucy had heard a flurry of clicks and high-pierced squeals as a pod of dusky dolphins surrounded her. They darted past, hundreds of them, their dark eyes fixed upon her. Lucy had grinned and started to sing through her snorkel, joy welling up inside her at this encounter. A mother brought her baby close, the little one inquisitive about this strange creature in their realm making funny noises. Lucy had felt a connection with these creatures, the part of her that was from the sea calling to them, wanting to swim as elegantly as they did, to dive down and then leap for joy into the air.

And then, all at once, they were gone, the pod moving on as fast as they had appeared. But the kinship she'd felt still warmed her inside.

"We're going onto Picton after a rest stop in Kaikoura," the driver said, noticing that Lucy was awake. "They can't take all the refugees. It's too small here, so we're moving on soon towards Wellington. I can take you all the way to the ferry if you like."

Lucy thought of what the Maori woman had said at the river last night. Was Amber here? She had to take the chance.

"I'll get out," she said. "Thanks for the ride, but I have to find my sister."

CHAPTER 11

"I DON'T REALLY HAVE a brother," Ben said.

"Yeah, no shit." Gina laughed. "Ben and Jerry? You're a terrible liar. But if you want to go in the caves, I'm definitely coming with you. It's not safe down there at the best of times."

Ben sighed, shaking his head. "Are you sure?"

"Yup." She grinned. "So what's in the caves anyway?"

Ben hesitated. "I don't actually know."

"You don't *know*? Hell, I always get mixed up with the wrong guys…"

Ben looked down at Gina. Her hazel eyes sparkled with humor in the torchlight. He wondered if he could trust her with the truth. The reality was that it didn't seem fair not to – Gina had no idea what she was signing up for with him. He had to try and explain, for her own sake.

"This will sound crazy, but there are these demons. More like gods perhaps, but demons too."

"Like monsters?" Gina frowned.

Ben nodded. "I saw one kill my grandfather, and I think the tidal wave and the earthquakes are related. I understand if you want to go back. I shouldn't have gotten you involved in this. But I have to go on."

Gina stepped closer to Ben and looked up into his eyes.

"And there's a woman involved, right?"

"Yes. Lucy. It's comp –"

"Complicated. Yes, it always is," said Gina. "So why the ice caves?"

Ben pulled the talisman from his shirt and held it out so Gina could see. The bone figurine glowed in the reflected light from the glacier.

"I have to get this into the ice cave. Deliver it to someone or something."

"And that will save the world?"

"Maybe. I don't know."

Ben tucked the talisman back into his shirt. Gina was silent for a moment, her head tilted to one side as she considered his words. Then she shrugged.

"It's definitely weird, but hey, I've done ayahuasca at Burning Man. I know there's more than a physical plane of existence. So I'm with you. As crazy as it is to deliver a talisman to a Tasmanian devil –"

"Maori god."

"Maori, Tasmanian. Whatever." Gina shrugged. "Let's go before I change my mind." She took a step down the trail to the right and then turned back to him. "You coming?"

Ben smiled, and they walked on.

The path wound down the side of the ice towards a rocky cliff face. They descended in silence. The glacier glowed with blue light as if lit from within, so they turned off the flashlight as they walked closer. The path opened up as it reached the entry to a cave, a tunnel of ice into the depths of the glacier. Swirls of soft blue and violet twisted through the white. Ben exhaled and his breath froze in the air.

He stepped inside the entrance, then turned back to Gina.

"Last chance," he said.

She moved ahead of him into the cave. "How deep you think we have to go?"

Her voice bounced off the smooth walls of ice and came back to them in a warped whisper. A *drip drip drip* sound joined her echo. Ben thought of the tourists crushed under tons of ice here a few years back. The glacier was always moving, ebbing and flowing over millennia. Nothing was solid here, yet the talisman drew him inward.

"We have to go all the way," Ben said. "We should put on more layers."

They opened the packs and put on padded coats, then attached spikes to their shoes. Gina's lips were blue with cold, but her eyes shone with excitement.

Ben took several steps deeper into the cave and felt a sudden tightening in his chest. He inhaled, yet it felt as though he couldn't get air deep enough into his lungs. He clutched at the wall as a haze of black smoke seeped from the ice, surrounding him.

The ice world shimmered. Gina seemed frozen in time, her form wavering as if she stood behind a waterfall. A cacophony hammered Ben's ears and he clutched at his skull in pain.

Then, suddenly it was silent. Ben stood in the middle of nothingness upon an invisible pedestal on a sea of black.

This is what the people hath wrought. Turn back.

The voice was the sharp edge of a knife, the dripping of blood, an ancient agony turned into sound.

As the sacrifice grows, my power increases. This is what must be.

His grandfather had told Ben many myths, but there was one that chilled his flesh to hear it spoken of. Whiro, god of darkness and embodiment of evil, lived in the underworld. He ate the bodies of the dead and gained their power. It was said that when Whiro became powerful enough, he would break free of the underworld, rise to the surface and consume the entire world. Whiro had taken his grandfather; now, he was here.

Anger rose within Ben. He would fight this demon with every breath left in his body. He grabbed the talisman and spoke a *karakia* of protection, the words taught to him by Tamati years ago. The dark creature in the smoke roared. As it sank its talons into his mind, Ben tried to scream, his mouth frozen open in pain as the world exploded into black.

***

A voice called to Ben in the darkness. He clung to the sound.

"Ben. Are you OK?"

He opened his eyes and saw Gina's concerned face. She squatted next to him on the ice, shaking his shoulder.

"You passed out for a minute. Here. Drink some of this."

Ben emptied the plastic water bottle, gulping the liquid down as he tried to push aside his fear. Whiro wasn't done yet, he knew that for sure.

They were running out of time.

"We have to get going," Ben said. He pushed himself up the wall on shaky legs, but after a few steps they felt stronger again and he strode onward.

As he and Gina descended, the blues of the ice turned into a deeper purple, with lines of black racing through it. The angle of descent increased and the cave walls closed in until Ben could touch both sides with arms extended.

Then, it narrowed even further.

"We have to crawl," he said, trying not to think of the tons of ice above them, the crushing weight of all that ancient frozen ocean.

"Keep moving," Gina said from behind him. "And pray it doesn't get any narrower."

Ben knelt down and crawled in. After a few meters, his flashlight flickered and died.

His heart pounded with fear. He wanted to bolt.

Only the fact that Gina was behind him stopped him from scooting backwards. The darkness overwhelmed him and he gasped for breath, trying to calm his claustrophobia.

Then, he saw a speck of light. It glowed like a morning star, casting rays of white through the glacier like a promise. He crawled on, faster now as Gina hurried to keep up behind him.

The tunnel opened out into a large cave. Stalactites of crystalline ice hung from the curved ceiling, forming spiked pillars like a huge cathedral. Gina emerged from the tunnel.

"This is very cool," she said, spinning around. "Some random demon church in the middle of the ice. You sure know some awesome places, Ben."

The pendant burned on Ben's chest and he pulled it from his clothes. It was ice cold, and he felt drawn forward through the cave. At the far end, an altar of ice rose from the cave floor. A piercing blue thread of light wound through the air. The light touched the pendant, and it glowed with inner power, pulsing in his hand.

Ben followed the blue light to the altar. He took off the pendant and laid it on top. The ice around it burned away and water vapor evaporated into the air. The pendant sunk down until it rested on top of a box hidden within the altar itself. The box was a match to the one the pendant had been stored in. Ben reached in and pulled it out.

Gina came up to stand next to him.

"Open it," she whispered.

Ben shut his eyes and thought of his grandfather. If Tamati had been here, he would have known what to do. Now Ben would honor his final wishes.

He opened the box.

Inside, a sliver of dried wood about five centimeters long sat on a pile of woven flax. Ben reached in and touched it. His grandfather's words came to him over the years, tales of the great *waka*, canoes that the ancient warriors had paddled from Hawaiki, the ancestral homeland, back in the days when the gods had blessed Aotearoa. The *waka* represented the people, a promise of safety over the waters and a new home.

Ben sensed that this wasn't the end of the quest. Perhaps it was only the beginning.

He reached in and took out the shard. It had a pinhole at the top, so Ben untied the string of the bone talisman and added the *waka* piece to it. He retied the string and put it back around his neck.

"And I thought men couldn't accessorize," Gina said.

Ben couldn't help but grin.

He slammed the box shut. The noise reverberated through the ice cave and the blue light around them dimmed.

A loud crack resounded in the cave and a crevasse began to open down the middle. Black smoke seeped out, consuming the light within the ice cave like a ravenous dog.

Whiro.

CHAPTER 12

THE KAIKOURA REST STOP car park was packed with vehicles of all kinds. There was none of the usual bustle from holiday-makers and tourists. There was only a bone-tired emptiness among those who leaned against their cars, faces fixed in survival mode. Two volunteers handed out bottles of water and boxes of rations from Red Cross vans. People took them in silence.

Everyone was heading north, away from the horror and devastation of the South Island. The majority of the population and infrastructure were in the north. The larger ports were north. There would be more help there.

Lucy wove through the crowd as she made her way towards what looked like some kind of administration tent. She heard snatches of conversation as she walked.

"I've heard the Aussies are rescuing people out of Wellington by boat. Maybe they'll take us, too."

"Thousands are dead in Dunedin. My cousin was there."

"Te Anau is completely buried."

"How could God let this happen to us?"

The last voice was desperate, pleading, unable to accept the reality of destruction. Lucy turned away, shutting her ears to hopelessness. She had to believe that Amber was still alive.

A ruddy-faced Maori woman shuffled lists in the administration tent, piles of paper stacked around her and a laptop on the table pinging messages every few seconds.

"I'm looking for my sister," Lucy said.

"Join the queue," the woman replied sharply. "Everyone's looking for someone, love." Then she looked up and caught sight of Lucy's pendant.

"That's unusual," the woman said, her eyes widening. "I've only seen that particular design once before … long ago." She came closer. "Who are you looking for again?"

"My sister, Amber Campion."

The woman turned to the laptop, typed in the name. Nothing.

She grabbed the paper lists and scanned through them quickly.

Nothing.

The woman shook her head. "Sorry, no one by that name is registered as coming through here, but to be honest, we're just trying to keep a semblance of organization in the face of massive disaster. We're meant to track everyone but not everyone registers on their way north. I'm sorry."

Lucy turned to go, but the woman grabbed her arm.

"Wait," she said. "You probably don't want to hear this, but I know there's a parallel route in place." She sighed. "It's always this way in disasters. There's those who help others in need and deny their own comfort, and then there's those who take advantage, using the chaos as a smokescreen for their own gain. There's only so much we can do, especially as the police and the military are overwhelmed right now."

"Gangs?" Lucy said with a frown.

The woman nodded. "And worse. I've heard rumors of traffickers picking up children. They stop near here to refuel before heading to the port at Picton."

Lucy's eyes widened in horror, her mind filled with images of what could be happening to Amber right now.

"There now. I'm sure your sister isn't among

them." The woman patted Lucy's arm. "But if you want to know more, go down to the Esplanade where the boats are. Keep that pendant out and proud and someone will help you."

Lucy touched the greenstone at her neck. "What's so special about it?" she asked, thinking of the old woman in the trees last night.

The administrator shook her head. "I can't say exactly, only that you will be helped."

Lucy walked out of the tent and headed down towards the Esplanade.

***

Rangi Anahera loved working the boats in Kaikoura, but it didn't exactly pay well. He did some jobs on the side, nothing too flash, and the money helped keep his mother and sisters going. He wasn't the best son, but at least he sent money back to the *whanau*.

Now, he sat on the back of a truck keeping watch, having a smoke. The truck had arrived in the early hours from Christchurch. The driver looked Indonesian, maybe Malaysian. Some kind of Asian anyway, with a name like Sitona. He'd thrust a roll of dollars at the yard boss and gone inside the office. Rangi knew they were negotiating, and that nothing good was going down right now.

Part of him wondered what was in the truck.

Part of him did not want to know.

The trucks with scorpion badges came through often enough, and they were never good news. The driver had said it was important that no one look inside, and Rangi's boss had nodded in that peculiar way.

So he wouldn't look.

Rangi was used to guarding things. He was a big man, and proud of it. Maybe some of it was fat now, but most of it was still muscle, honed by years working the boats.

He took another hit from the joint and inhaled deeply, imagining the smoke filling him, pushing out the parts of him that were scared. He couldn't show his fear outwardly. The others would finish him for it.

When the earthquakes had hit, he had been out on one of the tourist boats, whale watching – or at least scanning the ocean for a plume of water from the blowhole of a surfacing whale. That was all the tourists saw, really. He didn't care. It was nice enough to spend the day scanning the ocean. The time passed quickly and he loved the sea breeze, being out there close to the sky as the shearwaters dove for fish.

Moments before it happened an albatross had

swept in, gliding above the boat, its huge wings unwavering as it dipped down to look at the curious creatures snapping pictures. Rangi wished he could fly away like that bird and escape what he had become on land. Somehow the little jobs he had started doing years ago had morphed into things he knew were wrong now. The eyes of the *Toroa*, the wanderer, fixed upon him and he had felt convicted.

Then the wave came.

That terrible wave.

Rangi had stared straight into it and had seen creatures from the stories his grandmother had told, back on the *marae* when he was young. Back then, he had believed those myths. He had sat wide-eyed at tales of the Time Before. And in that wave, he had seen them again.

He took another toke, pushing the thoughts aside.

A young woman walked towards him along the road from the rest stop. Her blonde hair was bright in the sun. Only a few days ago, she would have smiled at the ocean, but now her face was set like all the others. She had a pack on her back and she limped a little, but there was determination there. New Zealanders were survivors, clinging to the edge of this violent land, and she was definitely no tourist.

As she walked closer, Rangi caught sight of the pendant around her neck. The greenstone caught the sun and he saw the head of the albatross in the *manaia* … And then, he saw the curl of the creature he had glimpsed in the wave.

The wave was in her. She was the ocean.

Rangi's eyes widened at the strange thoughts in his mind. He shook his head and dropped the joint, crushing it underfoot.

The young woman came closer, until she stood right in front of him. Rangi couldn't keep his eyes from the pendant. He should tell her to go away, but it transfixed him. The spirits swirled around this Pakeha girl.

"I'm looking for my sister," the young woman said. "Her name is Amber. I'm Lucy."

Her blue eyes seared into him and Rangi felt as if she saw right through him.

"I was told there might be people coming through down here," Lucy continued. "Do you know any-thing about that?" She looked pointedly at the truck behind him.

Rangi stood up, his six-foot-five bulk towering over her.

"There's nothing for you here, girl." Rangi spoke quietly. "You should go." He didn't want the Indo guy seeing her. She was pretty, not someone who should be out in times like these.

"I have to find her. Please. Do you know anything?"

As Rangi opened his mouth to speak, a banging came from inside the truck. The heel of a boot on the metal side panels.

"What's in there?" Lucy asked, her voice rising. "There's someone in there, isn't there?"

Rangi spun around. He had guarded plenty of trucks before, but none had sounded like this. If she spoke the truth, this product wasn't one he could let pass.

Lucy ducked under his arm and tried to tug the door open, but it was locked. Rangi grabbed a wrench and, with a mighty heave, he cracked the lock and slid the back door open.

There were kids in the back of the truck. They lay curled around each other, clearly drugged. Five of them – two girls, three boys. The youngest looked to be around four, the same age as his nephew.

Rangi felt sick to his stomach. Rage welled inside him.

This was enough.

"Amber," Lucy cried, scrambling into the truck.

Then all hell broke loose.

CHAPTER 13

BEN GRABBED GINA'S HAND and pulled her back towards the entrance.

"We have to go," he shouted. "Stay right behind me."

"No way," Gina said. She overtook him and dove into the tunnel first. She crawled ahead of him so fast that Ben struggled to keep up, even as he felt the icy fingers of darkness seeping after them.

As the tunnel widened, they ran upwards. The cave walls shook and crumbled. Chunks of ice fell down and the cracks became visible above and around them. The noise of disintegration, the creaking of shifting ice, the cracking of its seams, split the air.

"We can't make it," Gina shouted. "We can't outrun the collapse."

Ben grabbed her hand. Whiro would not take them here. Not while Ben still drew breath.

"Yes, we can."

He pulled her onwards. They ran left and right, dodging the falling ice as they raced up the tunnel. It widened further as they got closer to the exit, and then Ben caught sight of a speck of natural moonlight reflecting off the ice walls.

"We're almost there," he gasped, his breath almost gone.

"Ben, wait –"

He heard a cry as Gina slipped and fell on the broken ice. She rolled, her hip smacking on the hard ground. Ben turned back.

A deep rumbling came from behind them. He could see the tunnel collapsing, folding in on itself, swallowing everything in an icy tomb. Dark smoke rolled towards them, clawed talons stretching towards Gina on the ground.

Ben grabbed Gina under the arms, hefting her into a fireman's lift. She moaned as he ran, lumbering for the opening.

A hunk of ice fell. The sharp edge sliced open the flesh on his cheek. He ignored the burning pain and ran faster.

A sharp retort echoed through the cave as cracks opened up above. Ben ran through a mist of icy dust and leaped for the exit, hurling them both from the cave.

He landed heavily and Gina fell from his shoulder. Ben tumbled sideways as a deafening roar exploded from the cave. A hail of shards rained down upon them as the ice collapsed and buried the entrance.

After a moment, it was quiet again.

Ben sat up and brushed the ice off his skin. Gina lay unmoving next to him, her face turned away.

"Gina?"

Ben knelt next to her and put a hand on her back, rolling her towards him. She groaned and blew a lock of hair from her face.

"You really know how to show a girl a good time."

"Dammit. I thought you were dead."

"I'll probably wish I was tomorrow," she said. "Everything hurts."

Gina sat up and Ben leaned back, his legs folded beneath him.

"I can't believe we made it out of there," she said. "The military will be up here soon, though, after all the noise from the cave-in. We should go. Do you know where to next?"

"North," Ben said, feeling the pulse of the double talisman around his neck. He didn't know where yet, but it was definitely north.

"Well, that clears everything up," Gina said with a wry smile. "As long as there are beaches up there, I'm coming too. I'm done with the cold."

Ben stood and brushed the ice from his clothing, then helped Gina do the same. Together they stumbled away from the glacier, arms wrapped around each other.

Gina didn't say much as they headed back down the trail towards where they had left the truck. But then, Ben wasn't sure what he expected her to say. She wore her punk-rock attitude like a comfortable pair of jeans, yet what they had experienced was so bizarre that he couldn't imagine what was running through her mind.

"Are you alright?" he asked, the only question that seemed both safe and appropriate.

She took his arm and they stopped for a moment. The first light had appeared in the east, lighting the sky from beneath with a golden glow.

"This is some crazy shit, Ben."

"Yeah, I know. Sure you want to be part of it?"

"In a few weeks I'll be back at the coffee shop on Wacker Street. You think scaling ice caves and vanquishing smoke demons is hard? Try surviving a Chicago winter."

They laughed together as they stumbled back to the truck. Once there, they changed into warmer clothes and ate some of the rations.

"We need to get to the North Island," Ben said. "It's about eight hours' drive to the Picton ferry, so we can take it in turns and sleep on the way. I'll take first shift."

Gina pushed the passenger seat back, pulled her fleece jacket around her, and was soon asleep. As Ben pulled out onto the highway, his mind was filled with thoughts of smoke in the ice. It wasn't over yet, but at least he would make it further north.

CHAPTER 14

THE DOOR TO THE office across the yard opened and Sitona ran out. He pointed a gun at Lucy as he screamed abuse.

"Get out of there, you little bitch!"

Rangi saw the albatross in his mind's eye, the wanderer hovering over him, and he felt his spirit soar above the earth.

He stepped in front of the man and backhanded him to the ground with a powerful blow. The gun skittered across the yard.

"How dare you?" Sitona snarled. He rubbed his split lip as he tried to stand, blood dripping down his chin. "We have a deal."

"There's no deal if it involves kids." Rangi stepped in and kicked him in the gut, his thick-soled boots thumping against flesh. Sitona slumped on the ground, clutching his belly. He moaned in pain and rolled in the dirt. Rangi felt the adrenalin rush of violence, the part of him descended from Tumatauenga, the red-faced god of war.

"These are my people," Rangi shouted, his bulk towering over the prone man. "You pollute my land. The gods may be punishing us, but you cannot take our children."

He pulled a knife from his boot.

At the glint of metal, Sitona put his hands up in surrender.

"Stop! I'll let them go."

But Rangi saw evil in the man's eyes – evil done in the past, and evil in his future. Now was a time of vengeance in the land. Blood had been spilled, but not enough to assuage the anger of the gods.

They needed more.

He bent and grabbed the man's head, twisting it and wrenching it back. Sitona whimpered as Rangi held the knife against the pulse in his neck.

Rangi wanted to slice deep and fast. It would be just like killing a pig for the *hangi*. His breath came hard as he angled the knife for the cut.

But then he looked over at Lucy cradling her sister in the truck. He wanted to be part of the good in the world now. He was done with his violent past.

"Stay away," Rangi growled in Sitona's ear. Then very slowly, deliberately, he drew the knife across the man's cheek, deep enough that it would leave a scar. Sitona thrashed in Rangi's arms but he clenched the man's neck tighter and repeated the deep slash on the other cheek. Blood ran down Sitona's face, coating Rangi's hand and speckling the ground of the boatyard.

Rangi pushed the man away and Sitona fell back to the ground, clutching his wounded face.

The yard boss stepped out of his office. Rangi stood tall and proud over his whimpering foe, like a warrior of the olden times. His fists were clenched, ready to defend his actions. Ready to protect the children.

The older man looked at the truck where the children lay. Lucy hugged her unconscious sister, rocking her silently. After a moment, the man nodded at Rangi, assent in his eyes. He stepped back into the office and shut the door.

Rangi wiped his knife and put it back in his boot. He walked to the outside wash basin where they filleted fish every day and washed his hands, watching as the blood ran down the drain.

An albatross called high above him. Rangi looked up to see the great bird soaring in the blue, its wingspan casting a shadow on the bloody earth. He turned to the truck where Lucy sat, the *manaia* pendant around her neck. Something about it called to him.

He walked back to the truck.

"I can take you north," he said. "There are boats going over the Strait."

Lucy stared behind him at Sitona moaning on the ground. Her eyes hardened and then she looked up at him. There was no judgement there, only hope.

"Yes," she said. "I'd like that."

***

Lucy looked over at the huge man as they drove back up the hill towards the emergency station. His thick black hair was tied back with a leather cord and his goatee was neatly trimmed. Tribal and gang tattoos wound their way under the neck of a motorcycle t-shirt, emerging on his powerful arms. His nose was crooked and his ears mashed like a rugby player's. Lucy touched the pendant around her neck. What had he seen in it?

He was the type of man she would usually cross the road to skirt around, avoiding eye contact. The type of man she would never get in a vehicle with, let alone trust a group of children to. His dark eyes were fixed on the road, and there was a tension in him born of the violence he had inflicted. Lucy could still see traces of blood on his fingernails where he clutched the wheel.

"Why did you help us?" she asked quietly. "I don't even know your name."

"I'm Rangi," he said, not looking at her. "The kids …" He shrugged. "And things have changed." He looked out towards the ocean, shaking his head. "Everything has changed."

He crunched the gears of the truck as they pulled into the emergency area at the top of the town.

"I need to go and get the medics," Lucy said, her hand hovering over the door handle. She wondered whether Rangi would take off while she left the truck for a moment.

He turned off the engine and pulled the keys from the ignition, handing them to her. She met his eyes. Unexpectedly, she saw something of her father there. She didn't know why, but she knew this man would protect her.

"I'll check on the kids," Rangi said. "I'll need to carry them to the medical area anyway."

Lucy jumped out of the truck and ran to the Red Cross tent. It was packed with people, some sitting in a daze, others getting bandaged.

"I need help," she called as she approached. "There are kids here. They've been sedated."

One of the medics jogged over to the vehicle with her and began to check on the children, pointing out the ones that Rangi should carry back to the medical tent.

"Lucy," a thin voice called.

Amber was awake. Lucy jumped back into the truck and pulled her sister into her arms.

"I'm so sorry," she whispered into Amber's hair. Tears spilled down her cheeks. "It's alright. You're safe now."

Amber clutched at her, pale fingers weak from the drugs.

"We can help her at the tent," the medic said from the back door of the truck. "Your friend carried the other kids over there too."

Lucy looked out at the craziness of the rest stop, the vehicles backed up on the road coming into town. It looked like the whole of the South Island was heading north, away from the destruction. The emergency area was swamped with people desperate to find their loved ones. Now that Amber was awake, it was better to head north.

"We're going on to Picton as soon as we load up," she said. "Thanks for your help."

The medic jogged back over to the emergency center.

Lucy put her pack under Amber's head.

"You need to rest awhile," she said, "but we need to help other people as well."

A huge figure appeared at the back of the truck. Amber gasped and clutched at Lucy's hand. Rangi leaned in.

"Catch," he said with a smile, and tossed a Moro bar inside.

Lucy caught it and handed it to Amber, who tore off the wrapper and bit into the chocolate and caramel.

"This is Rangi," Lucy said. "He's taking us north."

Rangi met her eyes and nodded.

"I'll see you girls right," he said, and Lucy noticed how he kept looking at her pendant with respect in his eyes. She didn't know what would happen on the way, but she felt drawn north. Perhaps she would still find Ben … if he was alive.

She slipped out of the truck and went back to the administration tent. The ruddy-faced Maori woman was still juggling files and questions. She looked up as Lucy entered.

"Find your sister then?"

Lucy nodded. "Yes, and some other children, too. They're in the medical tent, so hopefully they can be reunited with their families."

"If they've got any left," the woman said, her tone dejected. "We've heard about another massive aftershock further south, and more quakes across Fjordland." She shook her head. "More refugees heading north."

"We're going on to Picton," Lucy said. "We've room in the truck for more people. Who do you want us to take?"

The woman shuffled her pile of papers, raising an eyebrow.

"Give me ten minutes. I'll send a bunch over."

Lucy walked back over to the truck to find Amber sitting up front in the cab next to Rangi. Her sister giggled at something he said and Lucy couldn't help but smile at the moment of normality. In the midst of chaos, it was still possible to laugh.

"Feeling better?" she asked as she swung in next to them.

Amber nodded. "I don't really remember much, though," she said. "I remember queuing with you in the square and then the quake. Then I ran … but that's it."

"It doesn't matter now," Lucy said. "That part's over. But we've got further to go today."

In the rearview mirror, Lucy saw a line of refugees heading for the truck. Their faces were masks of suffering, features sagging with exhaustion. Rangi hopped out of the cab and helped them into the back, loading water and what little supplies were available alongside them. When the truck was full, he pulled the door closed.

As he got back into the cab, Lucy handed him the keys.

"It's not too far to Picton," she said.

"True." Rangi nodded. "We'll take it easy, but

should be there by early evening to make the last ferry – if the weather holds." He looked out towards the ocean and Lucy saw his lips move in a silent prayer. He must have seen something out there, too.

The road out of Kaikoura hugged the coastline as it wound north. The sound of the truck's engine was soothing. Amber rested her head on Lucy's shoulder and was soon asleep. The refugees were quiet in the back, and Rangi's eyes were fixed on the road. The sun on the water to the east was glorious, the ocean calm. It was almost as if nothing had happened.

Lucy reached for the pendant around her neck and held it, feeling the curves of the *manaia*. The messenger spanned the transition between the realms. The country felt as if it were in that between-place now as well, a limbo poised between life and death, creation and destruction. The primeval forces that welled up beneath the earth, cracked it open and split it apart, also renewed and reinvigorated. New Zealand had ever pulsed with the movement of tectonic plates, and it seemed that the land cared not for those who walked upon its crust. Lucy clutched the pendant more tightly. But perhaps the spirits did care, and wanted the people gone. It certainly felt that way right now.

Rangi turned on the radio, keeping the volume

low. Lucy listened, but she felt a separation from it all now, a sense that the whole world only existed in this truck, in each kilometer they traveled. The reports of destruction across the South Island seemed unbelievable. The numbers of the dead and the lost were abstract in their size.

Her mind couldn't take in any more.

Lucy recognized signs of shock, post-traumatic stress and fatigue in herself, but there would be time for collapse later. Once they were safely on a boat heading for the North Island, where things sounded better, she would sleep.

The road turned inland towards Blenheim as it reached the shoulder of the South Island, and Rangi drove carefully as they navigated the route. There were fewer vehicles than Lucy had expected. The area was sparsely populated, but she had thought more might have made it north out of Christchurch and the south. They rumbled through Blenheim, people staring up at the truck as they passed, until they crested a hill that looked down on the town of Picton.

Two large ferries were docked in the marina. Even from this distance, Lucy could make out soldiers herding people onto the boats. A flotilla of medium-sized vessels was moored nearby, and it looked like they were being filled up as well. The harbor was a hive of activity, but the bustle was welcome. Movement meant life. Lucy felt a wave of hope as they descended into the town. She shook Amber awake.

"Look," she said. "The ships are here. We'll be safe soon."

The sisters embraced and Rangi smiled broadly as they drove down towards the docks.

***

Back in Kaikoura, Sitona winced as the woman stitched the wounds in his cheeks. She was thin and he could see bruises and track marks on her arms, but she had a light touch. It was better than being handled by those tattooed gang bastards.

"Here," she whispered and handed him a mirror. "It's the best I can do."

Sitona looked at his reflection. His smooth coffee skin was marred by two bloody slashes, the skin around them red and puffy, his eyes bruised, his lip split in several places. He wasn't vain, but he knew his work had been easier because he was young, reasonably good looking and therefore considered trustworthy. But now that animal had ruined his face, he'd have to take the shadier work. More than that, those kids would have made him a fortune and now he had nothing.

Less than nothing.

Sitona thought back to the brief conversation with Juno. His cousin was no longer concerned about his safety and his tone had been cold and distant. Sitona knew he needed to make up for his failure.

He'd heard that the big Maori, Rangi, was heading north with two girls. The bitches would be enough to save his reputation and make some cash.

Sitona smiled, his ruined face a grimace in the mirror. Rangi would pay for what he had done.

CHAPTER 15

"Get in line!" the soldier barked at the crowd. His fingers drifted towards the gun on his belt. He gestured violently at a car that was trying to push into the queue of vehicles heading into the belly of the last ferry. Tempers frayed here at the crossing even in good times, and Lucy knew it would only take a spark to set off trouble now.

"Just gotta take your time, mate," Rangi said quietly, so as not to wake Amber, who had drifted off to sleep with her head against his warm bulk. His hands rested gently on the steering wheel and his calm demeanor permeated the cab of the truck. Lucy smiled at how Amber lay against him. She was certainly grateful for the big man right now.

She wound down the window and poked her head out, looking back along the road. The line of vehicles stretched as far as the edge of town now. In front of them, the cargo vessels were quickly filling up.

"Do you think everyone will get on in time?" Lucy said. "We have to get out of the harbor before the tides change."

"They'll have more ships coming, for sure." Rangi nodded towards Picton harbor, where boats of all sizes bobbed on the waves. "New Zealanders are water people. Up in Auckland, they have more boats per capita than anywhere else in the world."

Lucy grinned over at him. "We're nowhere near Auckland, though."

"True, but there's enough down here for us lot. It looks like they're forming a flotilla of the smaller boats to cross over with the protection of the larger ferries. Guess they want as many people out of here before dark as possible. There will only be more refugees tomorrow."

They didn't speak of the depth of destruction left behind, the South Island cities that had been crushed in the massive forces welling up from the earth and rolling in from the ocean.

The people who were lost.

There would be time for grief when they could be sure they were safe.

Lucy looked up at the sky. Dusk painted the clouds with hues of flamingo pink, tango orange and rich emperor's purple. The beauty was even more dramatic because of the dust in the air, the remains of those blown apart in the disaster as they headed back to the stars where they'd begun.

She realized that they would be out on the Strait as darkness fell, out in what many considered to be the most dangerous and unpredictable waters in the world. The Strait had strong tidal flows, unusual in their phasing. High waters met low, resulting in fluctuating currents and capricious surges. Death was a constant companion here, the dark side of this stunning setting, taking down those who disrespected the natural forces that controlled this place.

A shiver ran down Lucy's spine.

The Marlborough Sound was a glorious place to sail and explore above and below water, but it also called many to its depths. She remembered hearing about the French Pass scuba-diving incident, which had happened not far from where they sat. With the fastest tidal flows in New Zealand, it wasn't a place to be underestimated. Six scuba divers had been caught in a whirlpool that dragged them down ninety meters into Jacob's Hole and then pushed them violently back up to the surface, resulting in three deaths.

"Looks like we're in," Rangi said, breaking Lucy's pattern of thought. He grinned as the line started moving. "Next stop, Wellington."

He revved the engine and pulled forward onto the ferry with the next batch of cars, parking up close to the vehicles in front. Once they stopped, he jumped out and pulled open the back of the truck. Lucy ran around to join him, helping the refugees clamber out. She wondered how many of these people she would ever see again. She was sure there would be a procedure for refugees in Wellington, and they would all be looked after. The dying woman in the steam back in Christchurch still haunted her, but here at least, she had played a small part in helping.

The tannoy buzzed, and a loud voice echoed through the ferry.

"Please proceed to the passenger decks. Complimentary hot food and coffee is available to all. The first aid station is on Level 2."

They left the truck and walked up the metal stairs to the highest level of the passenger decks. There was a sheltered cabin with windows all around, but Amber ran outside to stand at the prow of the boat. The wind whipped her hair about her face, and she closed her eyes to let the salt spray touch her skin. Lucy felt a moment of happiness to see her sister alive and well. Despite everything that had happened, they would make it through this and begin anew.

A deep sonorous horn blasted, signaling the ferry was on the move. The engines throbbed below and the boat set off, weaving its way around the intricate bays and inlets of the Marlborough Sound.

Lucy stood next to Rangi at the railing, his huge bulk sheltering her from the wind. She felt safe next to him.

"Do you have family in the North Island?" she asked.

Rangi nodded. "Cousins, yes, and other *whanau.* Haven't seen them in a long time, though. They're up near Lake Waikaremoana."

Lucy nodded. "My Aunt Jenny is in Auckland, so I guess that's where we'll go. Our parents …" She made sure Amber was out of hearing range. "They died in Christchurch in the first wave."

"I'm sorry," Rangi said. "But I'll get you and Amber to your aunt." He turned to face her, his rugged face looking down, his deep brown eyes serious. "I promise."

The horn blasted again as the ferry finally reached the narrow channel between Arapawa Island and West Head, then moved out into the Cook Strait heading east towards Wellington.

"Raukawa Moana," Rangi said, his eyes fixed on the open ocean. "That's what we call this Strait. It means something like sea of bitter leaves."

He fell silent. Lucy listened to the ocean, the slap of waves on the hull, the rhythmic throbbing of the engine. Ahead of them they could see more of the flotilla, another large ferry and a number of smaller fishing boats, all crammed with people desperate to get to the North Island, away from the disaster in the south.

The boats were well lit and, as darkness fell, the twinkling lights had an almost festive feel. Families smiled as they drank hot chocolate in the shelter of the boat, their basic needs met and wounds tended to. Hope flourished again in the warmth of the evening. Some people even began to sing.

Then the wind shifted.

A smell of rotting fish and the stench of the dead rolled towards them. Clouds formed above the flotilla. A mist rose in the semi-darkness, cloaking the boats, hiding them from the land at either side of the Strait. The mist rolled onto the decks, a thick miasma that seemed almost alive as it touched them, clammy on their skin.

Lucy felt Rangi stiffen beside her. Amber came running back from the prow, huddling close between them as the mist swirled around. The three of them stared out towards the flotilla in front, hands gripping the railing as they waited, hearts pounding. Lucy felt nauseated and she swallowed down a revulsion that twisted her stomach.

Something was coming.

The waters began to boil around the flotilla, churning foam and spray into the air. Shouts rang out as the sailors tried to regain control. The boats rocked, the smaller ones spinning in a sudden vortex, smashing against each other. The crash of waves intensified, but couldn't drown out the screams of those on board.

The engine of their ferry reversed and the revving grew stronger as the skipper fought against the pull of the whirling waters before them.

Regardless, they were drawn ever closer to the floundering boats ahead.

Suddenly, a massive tentacle shot from the water, purple, thick and fleshy, covered with suckers lined with barbed hooks. It wound around one of the smaller boats and crushed it with one pulse, splintering its hull before it dragged the bulk of the craft under.

Some aboard jumped into the water, clambering onto what debris they could reach. Dead bodies floated around them, more popping to the surface as the sea churned.

The dark mist broke, opening up to the heavens above. The sky clustered with bright stars, the deep blue of almost-night. There was a moment of calm.

Seconds ticked by, and Lucy wondered if she had imagined the creature.

Then a low whistle came in the mist, as if something called to the deep, summoning the creature again. The sound made Lucy's skin crawl, like maggots erupting from a rotting corpse.

Black clouds swept over the stars and a thick curtain of rain descended on the boats, pounding down from the sky above, punishing the ships with stinging blows.

Lucy and Amber ran for cover, huddling under the shelter of a lifeboat. Rangi wrapped his arms around them and held them close, anchoring them even as they witnessed what unfolded before them.

The waters churned and frothed, spinning the boats ever closer to one another. Massive tentacles shot out of the water again, two of them whirling, barbed hooks visible even in the heavy rain.

They slammed into one of the bigger boats.

It heeled over under the creature's weight and then flipped upside down, trapping all those on board under the waves.

Lucy gasped. Amber hid her face against Rangi's side.

The tentacles emerged again, feeling up the side of the other ferry, the twin to the one they rode aboard. *Surely it can't take down such a big ship?* Lucy thought. *Please, no.*

More tentacles emerged, until all eight were

anchored at points on the ferry. Then the bulk of the giant octopus lurched from the sea, its full weight hanging from the side of the ship. Men emerged on the decks, hacking at the tentacles, using whatever they could find to try and dislodge the creature.

But it was too much.

The ferry listed, and began to sink sideways towards its foe. The screams of the damned pierced the drumming of the rain.

"What is it?" Lucy said, her voice weak with horror.

"Te Wheke-a-Muturangi," Rangi whispered, his eyes wide. "It is a *kaitiaki*. A guardian spirit of this crossing not seen since the Time Before." He turned to Lucy. "It will come for us next."

CHAPTER 16

"You must ask for help before Te Wheke comes," Rangi shouted. His voice could barely be heard above the raging storm and the crunching of metal as the ferry before them began to split. "We'll end up in the belly of the ocean if Tawhirimatea, the god of storms, breaks us apart. His anger is only just beginning."

"What do you mean?" Lucy said. "These are not my gods."

"Your pendant," Rangi pointed to her neck. "It's a powerful *taonga*, a treasure. Even though you're Pakeha, it was given to you for a reason. You may not know our gods, but they know you." Rangi turned and pointed towards the unfolding massacre. "Look at that. How would you explain it? Your culture has the kraken, the great sea monster that pulls ships down to the depths. That is our kraken, but it is not of this earth. We cannot defeat it with earthly things."

"Please, Lucy," Amber whispered. "Do something."

"I don't know how," Lucy said. She pulled the pendant out of her clothes, clutching the *manaia* between shaking fingers. "You should take it." She began to pull it over her head, wanting to give it to Rangi.

He stopped her with a strong hand.

"No. This is yours, for a reason that has not been revealed yet. But my grandmother told me stories on the *marae* years ago about the tests that the gods set for those in the old times. Perhaps those times have come again." He met her eyes. She saw fear there, but also trust in her and a belief in something much bigger than their tiny lives. As she clutched the pendant and opened her mind to possibility, she felt a soaring inside.

In her mind, she was lifted up into the sky, above the destruction. She could see her body below, frozen against the side of the lifeboat alongside her sister and their protector. She could see the giant octopus as it tore apart the ships that dared cross its path. Sea creatures swam below it, the silver flash of sharks feeding on the dead. The blood of sacrifice boiled in the water. Lucy felt the anger of the gods as it rippled through Aotearoa, causing the land to buckle and the seas to rise.

And she felt a tug of fire that ran north towards the volcanoes of the North Island. This was not yet the end, not for her and not for the people of this land. There was still a mighty reckoning to come.

But then she felt a blossoming inside, a tiny seed of hope, a warmth that spread through her body.

The earth itself did not want this all to end. She who gave birth to all things, Papatuanuku, the earth mother, the goddess, wanted restoration. Lucy felt a lightness inside, a kinship. Her family may have come to New Zealand later than the Maori, but her fierce love for this land bound her to it. Her blood ran with the rich earth of the south, the magma of the north, and the salt of the ocean that surrounded these islands.

In her mind, she asked the goddess for help. She called out from the depths of her soul, pleading for the people and the very earth they walked upon. She begged for mercy, and offered herself instead.

Take me, she whispered. *Let the others live.*

A whisper came on a warm breeze. *Go north, child.*

Suddenly, Lucy was back on the cold deck.

She was down on her knees, coughing and spluttering as the rain hammered down. She still clutched the pendant; it pulsed warm in her hand. She looked up into Rangi's dark eyes. He nodded at her, understanding sparking between them.

A sudden wind blew up, coming off the land to the south. It swept the mist and rain away and spun around the ships. As the air touched it, the giant octopus shuddered and pulled away from the ferry, slithering back into the ocean, retreating to the depths. The boiling of the waves subsided. Soon, all was still on the water again.

Those on the remaining ships thronged the decks. They looked down at the wreckage of the broken boats, the dead bodies that floated now on gentle waves. Sounds of sobbing came across the water as they mourned for those lost. Many more stood dry-eyed, silent as they bore witness.

The tannoy crackled and buzzed.

"This is the captain speaking." The man's voice broke, and there was a moment of silence before he continued. "We have witnessed truly terrible things tonight, but there's no time to stay and bring those lost onto the ships. We have to get you to Wellington in case … in case anything else happens. But be assured, there will be boats out tonight to collect the dead and lay them to rest. We'll be in Wellington within the hour."

Lucy, Amber and Rangi sat on the deck, remaining in their huddle by the lifeboat, arms wrapped around each other as the lights of Wellington drew closer. The capital city of New Zealand, surely it could shelter them before they headed north. Lucy sat wondering at the touch of the goddess, clinging to a warmth she could still feel inside.

But she also remembered the anger, and the vein of fire under the earth that ran north before them.

***

The boat limped through Fitzroy Bay and into the harbor, finally docking with a clunk of metal. Shouts of the crew rang through the night air. The familiar sounds roused the passengers, who began to gather their things.

Lucy stood up and stretched her arms and back as Rangi helped Amber to her feet. They all remained quiet as they queued to go back down to the vehicle deck. There was no pushing, no boisterous behavior, even from the children. People were blank-eyed, stunned by what they had seen. Had it really happened? There was a palpable sense of grief in the air, adding to the layers of suffering that these people already held within. But once again, there was no time to stop and think, no time to grieve.

Lucy helped Amber into the truck and jumped in beside her. Rangi revved the engine and pulled forward with the other vehicles. They passed foot passengers, their heads down as they walked from the boat. Lucy scanned their faces, watching for some who had traveled in their van, hoping that they could find safety here. She didn't recognize any of them, but she understood the heaviness in their steps. She felt an echo of it in her own soul, but Amber kept her going. She had to get her sister somewhere that would be safe, and then she would go north. Lucy felt the ticking of time passing. Every second was one closer to the end.

"I'm fine to keep driving," Rangi said. "I think Wellington will be packed with refugees from the south, so we should move on."

"I can drive on a second shift," Lucy said. "Let you get some rest later."

Rangi nodded. "I'll give you a nudge in a couple of hours. You should sleep. That was a hell of a crossing."

Lucy leaned against the side of the truck and placed her coat under her head for padding. She pulled Amber closer so her sister was tucked against her body, sharing warmth between them. Amber's breathing shifted quickly into sleep, and Lucy let the sounds of the road lull her as she stared out into the night. As she closed her eyes, she felt the warm wind from the south surround her, blowing away the nightmare creatures of the ocean.

CHAPTER 17

"BEN, WAKE UP. YOU'RE having a nightmare."

Ben blinked and opened his eyes. The sun streamed in through the window and warmed his face. Gina had one hand on the steering wheel and the other on his shoulder.

"I'm up," he said. "How long was I asleep?"

"Most of the ride. Nothing exciting. Just a steady stream of vehicles heading north. Anyone with a ride is hoping to get to Wellington. I'm not sure why people think things are better on the North Island, but…"

"But we have to go too."

"There's some traffic ahead," Gina said. "Well, not traffic like Chi-Town traffic, but probably congestion for the Aussies."

"Kiwis," said Ben. "New Zealanders are Kiwis."

Gina tossed a smile at Ben while tucking her hair behind her ear. "You're fruit."

Ben laughed and her light humor banished the last of his dark dreams.

"Is that Picton ahead?" she asked.

Ben gazed out the front of the windshield at the spectacular view unfolding before them. Queen Charlotte Drive took them down towards the shoreline, where Shakespeare Bay kissed the pristine, white beaches. With the Whenuanui Bay Scenic Reserve to their back and the coastal town of Picton ahead, the scene looked almost normal.

Lush, green mountains cupped the beach in its hands and the brilliant white sails of moored boats sparkled in the sun. Ben wanted nothing more than an afternoon exploring the bays from the water. But as the truck wove down Queen Charlotte Drive and came closer to Picton, he saw that the town had not escaped the chaos.

Troops bordered the roads leading into Picton and drab olive military vehicles dotted the streets. As they drove east on Dublin Street, the remains of a tidal surge became evident. Hunks of debris lay piled on the street, where the water deposited it on its way back out to the ocean. Cars sat stacked in piles, and some buildings had been pushed completely off their foundations. A bulky freighter sat in the bay, a lone dark blotch on the glassy blue water.

"Something happened here, too," Ben said. "Although it doesn't seem to be as bad as it was in the south. Head for the ferry terminal." He pointed at a sign with a boat on it.

Gina turned left and cruised north. Several times she had to swerve around old tires and hunks of cinder block. Dozens of other vehicles sat parked on the side of the road, abandoned by those who had already crossed to Wellington. People hurried towards the ferry port, all of them clutching what little personal belongings they could carry.

Gina stopped the Jeep, killed the engine, and looked at Ben. He continued to stare out the window at the bay.

"We should go."

"Yeah," Ben said. "We should."

They had to go north, but part of him wondered whether if he left now, he might never return.

A soldier with an automatic machine gun used the barrel of it to rap on Ben's window. "Let's go. Last ferry to Wellington is leaving in five minutes. Might not be another one."

Ben stepped out of the Jeep and Gina came around to his side.

"Why's that?" Ben asked the soldier.

"You didn't hear?"

"Hear what?"

"Some sea monster, giant octopus thing, attacked the boats last night. A lot of people died."

"And you want us to get on the next ferry?" Gina asked.

"You can do whatever the hell you want. But if you don't get on that ferry in the next five minutes, you ain't getting off the South Island for the foreseeable future."

The soldier turned and jogged away.

"Follow me," Ben said to Gina.

He ran down the street, leaping over trash left in the road as Gina followed behind. A crowd had gathered on the dock, fighting to get on the ferry as the ramps were drawn up. One of the crew members stood high on the side with a megaphone.

"No more. We're at capacity," the man yelled.

The crowd of people surged forward, several falling into the water.

"You can't leave us!" someone shouted from the crowd. "You promised us passage."

The soldier who had told Ben they had only minutes to get on the ferry reappeared. This time, the muzzle of his machine gun was trained on the crowd.

"Too late," the soldier said. "Disperse."

"Where?" asked a man in the crowd to the right of Ben. "Where are we supposed to go?"

Ben leaned over and whispered in Gina's ear. "I've got an idea. Do you trust me?"

Gina nodded.

Ben smiled and took her hand. They ran around the dock to a small kayak rental shop at the end of the street. It was empty, a sign on the door saying that the owner had left to go north. It was unlikely that he would be back. Ben walked around the back of the shop. Behind a fenced area, several kayaks hung on racks. There was one he liked the look of, a tandem that looked oceanworthy.

A flash of memory, and he was back in Akaroa Harbor two years ago, the sun shining on the water as he and Lucy paddled their way out of the sheltered bay towards the Canterbury Bight. *Call that paddling, Henare?* Lucy laughed as she splashed him. He smiled at the memory, wondering where she was, trusting that she was still alive. For now, at least.

Gina walked up behind him.

"No way," she said. "Some giant octopus has already eaten a ferry and you expect me to paddle to Wellington? You've lost your mind."

"I know what I'm doing. I can get us across the Strait."

Ben pushed away his doubts. The problem with crossing the Strait wasn't the distance. It was the tidal flow, the wind and the changeable seas, and he knew that relatively few people had ever managed it. But the driving need to get further north was a pulse within him, and there was no way he could paddle it alone. He needed Gina. She was capable and strong. She would be fine.

"Come on." He flashed an infectious grin. "I thought you were over here for an adventure. Well, this is it – Kiwi style. I'll give you a tiki tour of the Sound."

Gina narrowed her eyes, and Ben could see hesitation in her expression. But then she nodded.

"I've done some kayaking before, back in the States. No whitewater, though. You sure we'll be alright?"

"It'll be sweet as," Ben said. He laced his fingers into the fencing, testing its strength. "Now, give me a boost."

Gina helped Ben over the fence and he jumped down into the yard. The kayak was lightweight and in mint condition. The rudder strings worked. Ben hefted it out of the rack and placed it on the ground. But they still needed other gear.

"I won't be a minute," he called back to Gina. "Just gonna look around."

He turned to the back of the rental place. Wrapping his fleece around his fist, he broke a glass panel, then reached in and unlocked the door. It creaked as he walked inside, and he headed straight to the front to let Gina in.

"You sure we should be doing this?" she said as she walked inside.

"I'm going to leave the guy a note," Ben said. "We'll itemize what we take. If he comes back, he can email me and I'll pay up." He looked over at Gina. "But seriously, based on what we've seen, d'you reckon he's coming back?"

"Humans are survivors," she said. "I wouldn't write anyone off yet."

Ben went to the front desk of the store and pulled out a pad and pen from a drawer.

"Exactly. So we take what we need and leave an IOU."

Gina nodded, turning to the well-stocked rails.

"Hmm. Well, if you're paying, I'll get myself some of the good stuff. We've been in these clothes long enough."

They soon had a pile of equipment and gear in the middle of the shop. Warm clothes, waterproof paddle jackets and pants, plus an extra pair each bundled up in a waterproof bag. Hats, gloves, life jackets and spray skirts as well as a first aid kit, spare paddle, flares, extra food and water in dry bags. Ben added a kayak sail in the hope they could catch some favorable wind, and a Garmin waterproof GPS.

He pulled a tidal chart from the desk, then looked at the time.

"We need to get a move on," he said. "It's best to cross at slack tide."

"I'll go get the truck," Gina said. "We need to get all of this to the waterfront." She ducked out of the shop and jogged off down the street.

Ben checked the equipment again to make sure they had everything they needed. With the chaos right now, they couldn't count on a coastguard rescue if anything went wrong. But it felt good to be heading to the water again. Even after the tidal wave, after what he had seen in the depths not so long ago, Ben hankered for the smell of the ocean, the feel of the water.

The sound of an engine came from outside. A moment later, Gina entered the shop again.

"Good to go," Ben said.

Together they loaded the gear and carried the kayak to the car, then attached it with bungee cords. They drove east through Picton, out to Waikara Bay, and parked near the shore.

They geared up in silence.

Ben glanced out at the grey choppy waters of the Sound. This place was paradise when the sun shone, but when the weather changed, nature's dark side emerged.

CHAPTER 18

"So how long will the crossing take?" Gina asked, her voice not quite as strong as earlier.

Ben hesitated.

"Um … well. It's about three hours to the end of the channel before we reach the open ocean."

"Then what?"

"That's where it's hard to say," Ben said. "At that point, we'll have to assess whether to abort the crossing or commit. Once we're out of the channel, we have to paddle hard for Wellington across the Strait. I know people who've done the whole thing in nine hours."

Gina froze. Her hazel eyes were wide, and her hands clutched her life jacket with white knuckles. Ben had taught kayaking and sailing back in Christchurch; he would have suggested that anyone with that expression stay on shore.

"Nine hours." She shook her head. "I was right – you really do know how to show a girl a good time." Then she grinned. "But hey, it'll be a hell of a story once I get back home."

Ben smiled. He walked over and gave her a hug. She returned it, wrapping her arms around his strong back. For a moment, Ben wanted to stay like that, their bodies pressed against each other. Thoughts of Lucy stole into his mind.

He stepped away.

"Thank you," he said. "I couldn't have made it this far without you."

"Sounds like we're only just beginning," Gina said, her voice soft. "Let's get going then, before I change my mind."

They carried the kayak down to the water's edge and packed it with the dry bags. They attached the other gear in front with bungee cords before getting in, Ben in front and Gina at the rear. They pulled on their spray skirts and pushed off from the shore, paddles dipping in unison as they rode the waves out into the bay.

Ben kept up a steady rhythm as they paddled east around the intricate bays of the Sound. His muscles registered the pull and push of the stroke, the dip and rise of the waves. The wind blew around them. The call of the gulls echoed above. Waves slapped on the hull.

Gina breathed evenly behind him, her strokes matching his. Ben's mind quieted as he took it all in, and his limbs became a meditation of movement. It felt good to be physically active again, every stroke taking him nearer his goal. The tug of the north pulled him forward and he let that energy wash through him, the cadence of the water flowing into his arms.

***

Eventually, they reached Arapawa Island, where only a small passage separated them from the Strait. Ben guided them into the shelter of a little bay where they stopped paddling for a moment, bobbing up and down. They caught their breath and drank from their water bottles.

"You OK?" Ben said after a few minutes of rest.

"Still good," Gina said. "I could murder a Mars bar though."

Ben laughed and pulled open his spray skirt, reaching down for the dry bag of food.

"I've got something better."

He handed Gina a massive Cookie Time biscuit with huge chocolate chunks and they munched happily, looking out at the bay before them.

"I wish I could have shown you this place at

another time," Ben said as the sun sparkled on the water. "You can spend days here exploring the bays, diving for *kai moana* – seafood – and fishing from the kayak."

"There'll be another time," Gina said, her voice certain. Ben wished he had her confidence.

"We'd better head out now," he said. "As soon as we pass the channel between the islands up there, we'll be in the Strait. Then it's full-on paddle."

"Good to go," Gina said.

They packed up the bag again, and Ben took up his rhythmic stroke, Gina matching him.

At the heads, Ben paused, looking out at the waters of the Strait. The waves were choppy out there, white caps frothing on breaking crests.

A fresh breeze, Ben thought. Not perfect conditions, but then they rarely were out here. He could see the North Island on the other side.

It didn't look so far.

They paddled on.

As soon as they reached the open Strait, out from the shelter of the bays, the wind hit them. Paddling was harder now; they rose up and down on the waves, sinking and rising with the water. The spray soaked them and, even with the extra clothes, Ben felt a deep chill sinking into him. He knew that the cold would soon sap their strength.

He didn't ask Gina how she was anymore. He kept paddling, staring into the waves, concentrating on each stroke, focused on the water.

The ocean was grey.

The grey of sharkskin.

Ben remembered the flash of the shark within the tidal wave, the story of the boats sunk by a giant octopus here last night. There would be predators under the waves right now, consuming the dead flesh of the victims. He remembered his grandfather telling the story of Te Parata, a monster of the tidal ocean who caused the high and low tides by swallowing vast quantities of water and then spitting it out again. Its mouth was a vast whirlpool, a watery abyss that devoured all who came close. Te Parata's resting place was near here.

Ben shook his head. All those stories. Were they just allegory, or was there an ancient truth beneath, something that was only now becoming apparent? From everything he'd seen in the last few days, he could no longer deny his grandfather's beliefs.

"I'm flagging," Gina's voice came from behind him, exhaustion clear in her tone.

"Stop paddling a moment," Ben called into the wind, turning a little in his seat. He reached into his life jacket for the GPS. They were barely over halfway and they'd been going for five hours.

He turned around, twisting his body in the kayak. Gina's face was pale, her lips a faint shade of blue.

She shivered a little.

"I don't know how much more I can do this," she whispered.

"I'm going to get us to shore," Ben said. "But you need to stay with me. I can paddle harder while you take a rest for a bit, but you'll be warmer if you keep paddling, even a little."

Gina nodded slightly. Ben felt a wave of guilt. He shouldn't have brought an amateur out here. But if they stopped for too long, they would be swept out into the ocean. On one side of the Strait was the Tasman Sea, with over 2000 kilometers to the Australian coast. On the other, the mighty South Pacific, all the way to Chile.

They couldn't stop.

Ben took a swig of water and refocused, putting every ounce of energy into his strokes, drawing on years of stamina on the ocean.

This is for Grandfather, he thought. *This is for Lucy. This is for Gina.* He repeated their names as the kayak glided over the waves.

After a time, a ray of sun broke through the clouds, lighting the waters ahead. Ben couldn't help but smile at the blessing and he heard Gina sigh behind him. She paddled again, buoyed by the sight, and they began to make better headway. The shore rose above them, getting closer every minute.

They managed for another hour before Ben felt Gina give up, but it wasn't much further now. He redoubled his strokes even as his muscles screamed for him to stop and rest. But after days of running in a country under collapse, of a life suddenly out of control, each stroke was his to win or lose. He forced his way onwards with gritted teeth.

He would get them to shore.

Ben willed himself onwards until eventually they inched their way past Taputeranga Island, finally landing on Houghton Bay.

He jumped out into the surf on shaky legs and dragged the kayak onto the stony beach. Gina fell out and collapsed in the shallow water. She looked up at him and shook her head.

"I'm never getting in a kayak again," she said.

"At least we didn't get eaten by the monster octopus."

Gina giggled, and Ben was glad to hear the sound. She would be alright.

Together, they crawled up the stones and lay looking up at the sky. The clouds gathered above but that was nothing unusual in Wellington. It rained a lot here.

Ben took a deep breath.

We did it, he thought. *Not even Te Parata could stop us.*

The pull of the north was stronger now. The talismans throbbed around his neck, and he could feel his own pulse against the hard stones of the beach. He had to keep going.

"Hey! You down there."

A strident voice came from the Esplanade above them.

Ben looked up to see a 4WD vehicle parked on the side of the road. An older bushy-bearded man stared down at them.

"Did you crazy buggers come across the Strait?"

Ben pulled himself to his feet. Gina stayed lying down, her eyes closed with exhaustion.

"We did," he said, walking over to the man.

"Then I want to shake your hand." The man shook Ben's hand vigorously. "I used to cross it back in my day, but it's been a long while since. I keep an eye out for those who do it though, especially in these dark times. Come. Call your girl over. I've hot coffee in my car and some banana bread."

Gina sat up at his inviting words and they gratefully accepted the hot drink and sweet cake from the man as he prattled about tales of his own crossings. Ben was grateful for the kindness of old explorers.

After recovering, they pulled dry clothes out of

the waterproof bags and got changed. Ben finally started to feel human again.

"Now, where you going next?" the man asked.

"We're trying to get north," Ben said.

The man shook his head. "Terrible times, you know. Lots of refugees heading to Auckland. The government have commandeered all the coaches and trains and are using them to take people on from Wellington."

"Any chance of a lift into town?" Ben asked.

"Of course." The man nodded. "Hop in."

CHAPTER 19

LUCY WOKE AS THE truck pulled into a service station on Highway 1 just past Palmerston North. She disentangled herself from Amber's sleeping form and rubbed her eyes.

"Sorry," Rangi said quietly. "I'm beat and don't want to drive when I'm this tired." He looked over at Amber. "Precious cargo aboard. We can stop if you like and both sleep."

Lucy shook her head.

"No, I'm good. I'll fill up with gas and get some supplies as well. You try to get some sleep."

Lucy clambered out of the truck, taking the keys from Rangi as he slipped into her place, gently rearranging Amber so she rested against his big frame.

The service station looked completely normal, a miracle after the last twenty-four hours. The lights inside revealed candy bars and bottled drinks and suddenly Lucy craved sugar and caffeine and normal things. She filled up the truck's tank and then went inside.

The night worker looked up as she came in, nodded at her, and then went back to the TV he was glued to. Lucy filled a basket with chocolate and crisps, Coca-Cola and some Lemon and Paeroa drink, Amber's favorite, although personally she couldn't stand the stuff. She took it all to the counter.

As she got closer, she saw the images on the TV: the wreckage of the boats on Cook Strait, illuminated by the bright spotlights of military helicopters. A series of images from Christchurch. Crushed and smashed buildings. Dead bodies in the streets.

The night worker shook his head.

"Terrible times, love," he said. "These are terrible times." He rang up the items. "You got far to go?"

"Not too far, I hope," Lucy whispered, her eyes fixed on the TV as her mind dwelled on the horror of what she'd left behind.

She paid quickly, grabbing the bag and hurrying back to the truck. She wanted to get as far as she could from the South Island. Lucy got back in the truck and pulled onto the highway, heading north as Rangi and Amber slept next to her.

It helped to focus on the road ahead, each kilometer passing by as the minutes of night ticked on.

The roads were dark out here, so only the headlights lit the way, illuminating the catseye reflectors in the middle of the road. As she drove, Lucy thought she saw shadows in the fields to the side, figures with arched spines and twisted limbs. They ran parallel to the truck, hungry eyes following her passage. But when she tried to catch a better glimpse of them, they faded away.

"Stay focused," she whispered to herself. "It's nearly over."

Soon, the road forked and Lucy turned east along the shoreline of Lake Taupo. The calm waters of the lake rippled with a slight breeze and she began to feel hope again. She remembered a holiday the Campion family had taken a few years back, before she'd left for University. Dad had bought her a tandem skydive, much to Amber's distress, although she'd been promised one when she was old enough. Lucy could still feel the exhilaration she had felt that day, tumbling out of the aircraft into the bright blue sky, looking down on this lake and the surrounding area as the air rushed past. It was over too quickly, but she would never forget that sensation of flying. She had felt something similar when sailing on the Moth as the dinghy lifted out of the water to plane on its hydrofoil. Lucy thought of Ben, hoping that he was alright out there.

The road turned at the very tip of the eastern shore and Lucy heard Rangi shift in the passenger seat.

"Lucy," he said suddenly, his voice tinged with alarm.

"What is it?" she said, glancing over to see his worried face.

"Amber," he said. "She's cold and her breathing isn't right."

Lucy felt a chill, her skin goose-bumping as concern shot through her.

"I'm pulling over."

She swerved onto the hard shoulder of the highway, headlights shining into the darkness of the fields around them, where she sensed unseen shadow figures lurking at the edge of the light. Lucy leaned over and felt Amber's forehead. Her sister's skin was clammy, like the mist that had swirled around them on the ocean. A sense of foreboding filled Lucy. Could the mist have somehow infected them?

"Amber." Lucy shook the sleeping girl. "Amber, wake up."

Nothing.

Amber's pulse was weak. Her breathing shallow. Lucy dug her nails into her sister's wrist, pinching her skin, hoping the pain would rouse her. There was no response. Tears pricked Lucy's eyes.

"Something happened on the crossing," Rangi said. "We need help."

"There's a hospital ahead in Taupo," Lucy said, her voice breaking as she tried to fight back the tears.

Rangi shook his head. "Not that kind of help," he said. "This is from the waters. The mist is inside her. But we can take her to my family. My grandmother, the *kaumatua,* will know what to do. It's a few hours' drive, but we can be there by the dawn."

Lucy nodded.

"I'll drive again," Rangi said. "You should hold your sister."

CHAPTER 20

Tongariro National Park Volcano Center,
North Island, New Zealand

CHARLIE FISHER TOOK A deep breath, held it for four seconds, and then exhaled slowly. He repeated the process several times, willing the panic to subside.

It had to be a mistake.

The readings must be wrong.

He looked again at the printouts in front of him. One part made sense. The seismograph showed tiny shocks followed by the spikes of the main event. He was used to that, even though he knew that the lines on the page represented huge catastrophe outside in the real world. It was strange that they hadn't seen this coming. There had been no warning. But then, the country sat on an active fault line between the Pacific Plate and the Australian Plate – tectonic shifts were part of living on the Shaky Isles.

But this …

Charlie reached for the second part of the printout. Earthquakes were one thing, but the North Island of New Zealand also had active volcanoes. This report showed the level of magma within Mount Tongariro.

It was rising.

Fast.

* * *

Deep within the earth, something massive shifted.

Rakahore, the god of rock and stone, had placed the sacred fire here in time gone by. While the children of the gods slept, the magma and molten lava heated the domain of those beneath, but as they woke, the chambers of superheated rock began to split and crumble.

Now Ruaumoko, the god of volcanoes and magma, forced his way towards the surface.

CHAPTER 21

THE OLD ADVENTURER DROPPED them off at the coach station, the only fare listening to his stories. Gina remained polite with a smile and an occasional nod, but Ben developed a genuine respect for anyone who had crossed the Strait. Multiple times.

They said their goodbyes and Ben led Gina into the station and onto the platform for the coach that would take them north. They were both exhausted and Ben was looking forward to sleeping onboard while they let the road take them north. Lines of refugees filled the station, all clambering to get on the coaches. A sense of desperation filled the air as they funneled towards the transport.

"Got your luggage?" Ben asked.

Gina held up the meager supplies from the kayak. "Of course. Everything a girl needs."

An announcement came over the loudspeaker and the crowd began to move.

"It's going to be cramped onboard," Ben said.

"As long as I don't have to paddle, I don't care," said Gina. "I'll be out like a light."

They boarded the coach and found seats together. Gina padded her head with the dry bag and was asleep within moments. An elderly Maori man sat across the aisle from Ben, his face lined with age and concern. He smiled, and Ben saw a trace of his grandfather there.

Ben relaxed into the warmth of Gina's body next to his and, as the coach pulled onto the road, he dropped into sleep.

When he woke up, the sun was lower in the sky. The old man gazed out the window, but turned his head as Ben stirred.

"Do you know what happened just before the eruption?" the old man said, his voice rich and deep.

"Which eruption?" Ben asked, struggling into consciousness.

"Mount Tarawera. In 1886."

Ben shook his head. The old man continued.

"Eleven days before, tourists from the Terraces saw a war canoe approach their boat. A local Maori from the Te Arawa *iwi* saw it too. He said the canoe disappeared into the mist. Nobody at the lake owned a war canoe, and nobody had seen anything like it before. Some believed it was an ancient *waka*."

Ben put his hand on his chest, where the sliver of wood hung. It burned his skin at the man's words.

"Some say an old burial *waka* came loose, or that it was nothing but a reflection on the mist. But others …" The old man wagged a finger at Ben. "They knew it was something else."

"What?" Ben asked.

"The tribal elders believed it to be a *waka wairua*, a spirit canoe. They say that when the spirit canoe appears, a volcanic eruption is coming – as it came at Mount Tarawera."

"*They* say a lot of things," Ben said, his words thin and unconvincing even to his own ears. "Maori stories are full of impending doom."

"Another *waka wairua* has been seen," the old man continued. "These times grow darker, my son."

He looked out of the window again, growing silent as they passed the national park. The cloud-capped peak of Mount Tongariro loomed to the east.

There was still time before the next rest stop at Rotorua, so Ben changed position and closed his eyes again, pushing away the old man's forbidding words.

* * *

"Rotorua! Rest stop time. Everyone off."

The loud voice woke Ben and he opened his eyes to find the old man had gone. He turned to Gina next to him. She had pulled a hoodie over her head while her cheek squashed against the window. She looked serene and Ben didn't want to wake her, but the bustle of the emptying coach made her stir.

"Are we nearly there yet?" she said, her voice fuzzy with sleep.

"Not quite in Auckland," Ben said. "But we need to get out. Mandatory rest stop and refueling. A chance for you to see Rotorua, the stinkiest place in New Zealand."

"I can't possibly miss that." Gina rolled her eyes.

Ben had been to Rotorua once before, but he had been so young that he couldn't remember much. It still stank of rotten eggs from the geothermal activity under the town. He hadn't forgotten that.

They got off the bus and immediately Ben could tell something wasn't right here. The expensive spas and lush landscaping remained intact, unlike what had happened in Christchurch, but the people in the town moved in furtive packs. Many pulled suitcases and carried bags in their arms, bundling their worry along with their most important possessions. The town was evacuating and barely in control. It felt like a slow-motion car crash, unlike the rapid disaster down south.

There was a bronze plaque by the bus station entrance. Ben read it silently, the words an ominous warning.

"… the fire demons dipped into the seas and each time they rose, they left a streaming trail of thermal activity behind them. That is the origin myth of Rotorua."

Ben turned to Gina, who had been reading the plaque next to him.

"This feels like some serious voodoo shit," she said. "Fire demons now?"

A shout came from behind them. Ben turned to see a plume of white, frothing steam explode from the earth.

Another explosion rocked the square, blowing earth high into the air as a second thermal vent broke open.

People who had been calmly stepping off the bus now ran for the nearest building. Those on the street scattered, looking for cover beneath anything that would protect them from the scalding water now coming down like rain.

"This way." Gina dashed across the road away from the steam, her arms up to protect her face.

As she stepped out, a bus came flying through the intersection. It slammed on its brakes. Gina made it across, but the bus blocked Ben's path. The doors opened and a mass of people spilled out, shouting and pushing in desperation as they fought their way to shelter.

Ben fought upstream against them, trying to get around the front of the bus where he had last seen Gina. Terrified cries filled the air as people ran, desperate to find a safe haven.

The fissure in the road split open. A popping sound filled the air, echoing like thunder through the street. Plumes of white water burst through the surface as more dormant geysers came back to life.

"Gina," Ben shouted, but his words were drowned out by the engine noise and the screams of those around. "Gina, wait."

Ben ducked and dodged. He slid around the front bumper of the bus and emerged on the other side of the road. Mobs of people filled the street. Ben scanned the tops of their heads, looking for purple highlights in blonde hair.

He pushed people aside and made it to where he had seen her last, right before the bus stopped in the middle of the street. Gina was gone.

He is coming and the fire demons are coming with him.

The voice echoed in Ben's head. It sounded like his grandfather, and yet, it also sounded like a chorus of lost souls, as if those in the beyond were trying to warn him.

He had to find Gina. He couldn't lose her now.

Crowds of people scurried by, changing direction as each thermal geyser exploded. Ben could sense power bound deep in the earth. It strained against the surface, its chains loosening as the ground shifted.

"Gina!" Ben kept shouting, although it was like calling into a hurricane. Between the screams of frightened people and the thermal activity, she wouldn't hear his calls no matter how close she was.

Ben jumped up onto a lamp post and climbed above the crowd. He scanned around – and there she was. A flash of purple. Gina was caught in the crowd moving as a herd south on Fenton Street.

Then, he saw something else.

His skin crawled as wisps of black smoke emerged from the drains. Its spidery tendrils wrapped around those in the crowd, stoking the terror of the mob.

Whiro.

"No," Ben whispered, as the dark strands reached towards Gina.

CHAPTER 22

RANGI CLUTCHED THE STEERING wheel with tight fists and focused on the road in front of him. It had been many years since he had driven this route, and far too long since he had seen the *whanau*, his extended family. He should have come north for the *tangi* – the funeral – of his uncle last year. It would have been the right thing to do. But he had been deep in gang business then, and the family gathering had seemed less important than another shipment, another dollar … another drug-filled party, if he were honest. But he was well over that life now.

He glanced over at Lucy. She stroked Amber's hair as she held her sister close. That kind of love seemed alien to Rangi, but it called to something deep within him. The last twenty-four hours had changed everything. It was only now, as the kilometers passed in the night, that he could consider what had happened.

It seemed as if the tales his grandmother had told him were coming to pass. Seeing Te Wheke in the waves, feeling Tawhirimatea, the god of storms, on the crossing. Things he had considered legend were real – and that changed everything.

Now he felt the call of his *iwi*, his tribe.

Even if they rejected him because of his past actions, they would take Amber in. He knew that they would help her because of the pendant Lucy wore. Rangi felt the throb of its power even now. Its tendrils wrapped around his heart, calling for his allegiance, holding him to a promise he didn't even know he had made. He would play his part in whatever came next and he would protect Lucy, whatever it took. However far they had to go.

A sign loomed in the dark and Rangi turned down State Highway 38, heading southeast towards the Kaingaroa Forest and on to Urewera National Park. As he drove into the forest, he opened his window and breathed in the scent of his home. This was old country, rugged and rooted deep. Rangi remembered trekking here with his grandmother back when he was a boy. Miles from anywhere, when he'd thought they were lost, they had emerged into a copse of silver beech. The cluster was known as a 'cloud forest,' and whipped by the wind over years, the trees had become stunted and dense. Their branches reached towards the sky like goblin fingers, draped in mosses and ferns. It was a fantasy place where he had felt the presence of the gods. He wondered if he could find it again someday.

The chirp and whistle of a *tui* echoed through the trees and then other birds joined in, the chorus of the forest. Rangi felt a rising joy within him, a happiness he hadn't felt for so long.

He was home.

As dawn broke, they emerged from the forest onto the bank of Lake Waikaremoana. A light breeze rippled the waters of the huge lake and a fine mist hung like spun sugar around its edges. Lucy sat up and looked out across the water.

"It's not far now," Rangi said. "We just need to go around the Lake and the *marae* is on the south side, near Tuai."

A few kilometers later, he pulled into the carpark outside a simple *marae,* a protected enclosure surrounding a wooden meeting house. The heart of the Maori community. There were a few houses nearby, but it was a small settlement. Some round here worked in the national park and the tourist industry locally, but most went east to Gisborne and the opportunities of the bigger cities of the North Island.

Rangi got out of the truck and stretched his back and legs, letting the early morning sun warm his limbs. Was this the right thing to do? The urge to bring Amber here had been strong in the night, when the spirits swirled about them, but now … now, he wondered whether he would even be welcome.

"Should we bring Amber out?" Lucy called softly from inside the truck.

"Wait a minute," Rangi said. "Let me go find my grandmother. She'll know what to do."

He walked around the edge of the *marae* to a small house. The red door was faded and scratched, but the plants in the garden were blooming and well kept. He smiled. His grandmother, Aroha, still had her priorities right.

Rangi knocked at the door. His heart pounded. What if she turned him away? What if she slammed the door in his face? She certainly had the right to. He had not been a good grandson.

The door creaked open.

Her brown face was more wrinkled now, the lines deeper, etched with the pain of her people and the weight of responsibility for this *hapu,* the extended families of the area. Her dark eyes narrowed a little, focusing on his face.

Then she beamed as recognition dawned. She flung the door open, her arms wide.

"Rangi," she said. "Welcome home, my boy." Rangi stepped forward and embraced her, leaning down and holding her close. Tears pricked his eyes as the years of being an outcast fell away.

"Let me look at you," Aroha said, stepping back, holding his face in her hands. Her deep brown eyes stared into his, and Rangi felt her search his soul. He caught his breath as she raked him through. Then she nodded with a smile.

"It is as it should be. Now, where is this sick girl?"

Rangi didn't question how she knew. Aroha had always been able to see through the veil of what the world considered real, to what lay beyond.

"In the truck." Rangi pointed.

"Bring her into the *marae*," Aroha said. "I'll meet you in there once I gather my things." She ducked back inside the house.

Rangi jogged to the truck, opened the door, and lifted Amber from Lucy's arms.

He carried the unconscious girl into the *marae* compound. At the steps of the meeting house, he slipped off his shoes. Lucy followed close behind.

Rangi laid Amber gently on the ground and smoothed the hair from her face. Lucy curled up next to her sister.

"It's going to be alright," she whispered.

Rangi stood and looked around *Te Wharenui*,

the meeting house. It was decorated with carved wooden panels depicting the gods, woven mats in between each panel. Even in these desperate times, it was good to be back.

Aroha came inside with a woven bag in her hand.

"Welcome, child," she said to Lucy, kneeling down next to Amber. She touched the girl gently, feeling her forehead. Aroha's eyes closed and her lips moved as she whispered ancient words.

Then she stopped. Her eyes opened.

"Show me, girl. What is it you carry for the gods?" Her voice wavered.

Lucy pulled out the *manaia* pendant from her clothes.

"Do you mean this?"

Aroha gasped, her fingers flying to her mouth at the sight.

CHAPTER 23

Tongariro National Park Volcano Center,
North Island, New Zealand

"I CAN'T MAKE IT across, Charlie." A crackle of static broke up the next words.

The phone network was down across the country. The mountain team had CB radio, but that wasn't enough to help Charlie now. Frank had many more years' experience with the volcano. He knew the moods of the mountain. They had even joked that his blood ran with magma. But Frank couldn't get here – he was trapped along with so many others in Ohakune, dealing with the aftermath of the quakes that continued to shake the whole country.

Charlie scrolled through the news reports. The internet was in a frenzy of speculation about what was coming next. That peculiar mix of grief and morbid fascination, desperate for details of tragedy. People couldn't keep their eyes from a disaster, especially if they weren't directly affected. He imagined people shaking their heads in sadness as they sipped their caramel lattes in coffee shops on the other side of the world.

He scrolled on through the newsfeed. Scientists from across the world were getting their two minutes of fame, discussing tectonic plate shifts and how none of this was unusual on the Pacific Rim of Fire. Images of destruction repeated over and over. Shattered buildings and piles of rubble. Streams of people trying to get out from the worst hit areas, their faces marred by smoke and blood.

And he was all alone up here.

A bead of sweat rolled down his back. Was it really getting hotter? Or was it just the stress?

He checked the readings again. There were sensors all over Mount Tongariro, but they hadn't seen readings like this even when the Te Mari Craters had erupted in 2012.

Charlie logged onto GeoNet, the official source of geological hazard information for New Zealand. It contained the latest reports from all over the country, with lists of earthquakes and volcanic alert levels as well as scans of seismic recordings for each of the volcanoes.

Only yesterday, the front page of GeoNet had been all green, the alert levels at 0 or 1. Now, the team could not update the page fast enough. The listed quakes were updating every few minutes and the volcano alert levels were currently at 2: moderate to heightened volcanic unrest.

Charlie's finger hovered over the keyboard. The alerts should be a lot higher. He should report his readings immediately, but the country was already in such a state of craziness, adding fear of eruption might tip it over. Could the readings be wrong?

He stood to refill his coffee cup and stretched his aching back. He had definitely been sitting too long. Perhaps he should go and take a look at the main craters. Charlie ran his fingers through his sandy hair as the kettle boiled. He looked out the window. From up here on the mountainside, all looked calm and peaceful.

He made his coffee and took it to the door of the monitoring station. He opened the door and sat on the top step, taking a sip.

Charlie loved being alone. It was his natural state. His ideal day involved walking the park with a pack on his back, in sun or rain or snow. He could go days without speaking to another person, and he was acutely aware of the sounds of the mountain. But as he swallowed the coffee, he realized that it was too quiet, even for him.

There was no birdsong in the air.

No hum or buzz of insects.

The air was still and heavy. And there was something else unusual. Through the soles of his shoes, he could feel warmth.

Charlie put his hand on the ground. It was warm to the touch, and getting hotter. No wonder the animals had fled and the birds had flown away. As creatures so close to the earth, they knew when trouble was on the way.

But he couldn't leave. His place was here.

He was part Maori on his mother's side, and she had spoken of his *whakapapa*, his ancestry. They were descended from the people of the mountain, those who had once worshipped here. Before she died, his mother had said that people nowadays had forgotten where they came from. They didn't honor the old gods anymore. They had turned the mountain into a tourist hotspot, tramping and skiing on it, oblivious to the sacred nature of the ground. Perhaps now they would pay the price for such hubris, as man had ever learned his most important lessons.

The hard way.

Charlie went inside and typed swiftly into GeoNet, reporting on the seismic readings and his observations of the environment. He didn't stop to note the replies that arrived thick and fast.

He grabbed his emergency pack and jogged outside, where he mounted a quad bike, revved the engine and headed up towards the main crater.

The wind whipped through his hair as he sped up the rocky slopes, the power of the machine beneath him propelling him onwards. He should be walking, he should be feeling the earth beneath his feet, but there was no time.

As he crested the ridge, a plume of smoke belched up from the crater in the distance. The black ash erupted into the blue sky above. Charlie was transfixed. It seemed as if there were creatures in the smoke, ash-formed shapes that gazed down at the land beneath, as if they hadn't seen it for generations. They shifted with the wind, dispersing and then re-forming into animal shapes, then human figures, then grew and shifted into great lizard creatures. Charlie rubbed his eyes, trying to clear his vision, the rational part of his mind denying what he saw.

Then a deep rumble came from beneath the earth, like the rush of a train along a tunnel. Charlie had studied volcanoes with a passion since childhood.

He knew what was coming.

He killed the engine and turned to sit sideways on the quad bike. There was no time to escape. He fixed his eyes on the crater, wanting to witness that which he had never seen with his own eyes.

A roar of gas and power exploded from the crater. A blast of superheated air smashed into Charlie. He shielded his eyes, feeling his flesh burn, but the pain was nothing. He knew it would be short-lived. A tower of bright orange, scarlet and vermilion rushed into the sky, shooting towards the clouds before it fell, turning black as it crashed down.

It was so beautiful.

Charlie smiled, tears in his eyes as his lifetime dream was fulfilled: to see the mighty eruption of his volcano. As the burning hot ash rained down upon him, speckling his skin and tainting his lungs, Charlie spoke aloud a *karakia* learned from his mother years ago, a prayer to the ancient gods, asking them to allow him home.

The creatures in the flaming rock reached out for him as he closed his eyes for the last time and the lava engulfed his body.

BBC WORLD NEWS REPORT: BREAKING NEWS

THOUSANDS OF NEW ZEALANDERS have fled their homes after a volcanic eruption at 11:42am in the center of the North Island today. Mount Tongariro is a compound volcano in the Taupo Volcanic Zone and is one of the most active in the north. Ngauruhoe, a cone of the volcano, has erupted more than seventy times since 1839, but geologists are citing this latest eruption as the worst event in recent history.

"I heard a massive boom and when I looked up, the side of the volcano was burning and ash was raining down," said Mo, a forty-two-year-old retailer from the mountain town of Ohakune, who was on the main shopping street at the time. "We've all heard about the possible 'big one,' an eruption that could kill us all, so I went home, got my son and we left. We're heading north to Auckland, like everyone else."

All flights in and out of the North Island have been suspended as ash from the Tongariro eruption spreads across the country. Experts say that tiny particles of sand, rock and glass contained in the ash can clog aircraft engines. Fluctuating winds have already driven the ash plume east, with fears of it shifting north towards Auckland in the next twenty-four hours, further complicating the rescue operations already in place for South Island refugees. Civil Defense officials are advising people to avoid traveling, but instead, to stay indoors and tape up windows as much as possible.

The eruption happened only two days after a tsunami crippled Christchurch and multiple earthquakes hit the South Island. A total of 3410 people are reported dead so far, with thousands more injured and missing. Official figures continue to rise.

"We're worried that the tectonic activity will spread," Mark Jacobs, vulcanologist at Massey University, reported earlier today in a press conference. "The Auckland volcanic field has fifty-three volcanoes. All are dormant and the majority have only erupted once. But Rangitoto has erupted repeatedly and is due for another eruption within a short period, geologically speaking. The next eruption could be in thousands of years' time, but it could just as well be tomorrow."

CHAPTER 24

BEN WADED INTO THE stream of humanity flowing south on Fenton, towards where he had last seen Gina. He tried to dodge through the crowd, but the route was thick with people desperate for shelter. He overheard parents telling their children that everything would be fine. Yet Ben felt Whiro's anger in the pulse of the earth and the black smoke that whirled about them.

"Where's everyone going?" he asked a man beside him in the crush.

"The Institute of Technology," the man said, his eyes wide with barely constrained panic. "They have an emergency shelter, and they're trying to figure out what's going on."

At the Institute, security guards with earpieces directed people towards stairwells that led to the heart of the building. Maybe Gina was already there. He was about to go down the stairwell when he heard his name.

"Ben!"

He turned to see Gina, a wide smile on her face. She was against the back wall of the lobby. A steady stream of people moved between them.

"Stay there," he shouted, pushing against the tide towards her.

Ben shoved his way through, knocking a floppy-haired teenager to the side in his haste. He reached out his hand to her and Gina leapt at him, her arms pulling him close. He breathed in the scent of her hair. They clung to each other. A moment of calm in the chaos. She gave him one more squeeze and then pulled away.

"The bus," Ben said. "I couldn't –"

"It's OK," Gina said. "We're together now." She looked towards the stairwell. "Should we go down there with everyone else? Back in the States, they built these fallout shelters in the '50s. Most of the old office buildings in Chicago have them. You think that's what's down there?"

"I'm not sure." Ben clutched at the talismans on his chest. He was still drawn north, and he felt a sense of foreboding here. After seeing the black smoke winding around the crowd, he didn't want to be trapped in here with them as the angry gods clawed their way from the depths of the earth.

"We should keep going north." Ben took Gina's hand and they squeezed through the crowd towards a side exit. "So we need to find a car."

They made it outside and rested for a moment, their backs against the wall of the building. Gina turned and planted a soft kiss on Ben's lips.

"I'm glad we found each other," she whispered.

Ben's breath caught in his chest. He wanted to pull her closer, but … Lucy.

Gina was one of the coolest women he'd ever met, but his heart belonged to another.

"Gina, I –"

She cut off his words with a finger on his lips. "I know. There's someone else. But you and I are here right now. So let's find a ride outta here." She grinned and spun away. "I bet I can find us the coolest car."

Gina jogged towards the Institute parking lot. Ben watched her trim figure as she ran to the abandoned vehicles. If they had met at some other time or place, their relationship might have been different. He smiled as he watched her try the door handles of the cars, shaking her head dramatically, making a performance of it. Ben couldn't help but laugh at her antics.

"Found one," she shouted from across the parking lot. "This little Honda is unlocked."

Suddenly, the sky darkened.

A tornado of black smoke swept into the car park. Ben's stomach twisted with visceral fear. *Whiro.*

The earth vibrated and cracked.

The asphalt in the parking lot broke apart, the noise like ripping flesh.

"Run, Gina!" Ben shouted.

The windows of the Institute shattered with the force of the quake. Fragments of broken glass rained down on Ben as he darted away. Black smoke poured from the ground, enveloping Gina until Ben could hardly see her.

The asphalt folded and the fissure split the ground, heading right for her. The cars in the parking lot slid sideways as if a giant had lifted them.

Gina jumped onto the hood of the Honda as other cars smashed into it. She leapt off the other side and sprinted towards the edge of the lot.

"Go, go!" Ben shifted his direction, running to intersect with her path.

Before he could reach her, a roar came from underground and a massive tree fell down, knocking Gina over as the leafy branches descended. She rolled and made it back to her feet. She stumbled to the left and then broke into a run again.

The edge of the lot was only yards away.

Then, Ben saw what was behind her.

It was a pool of bubbling, boiling grey mud used by the Institute to measure geothermal activity. The sludge sputtered violently, sending thick globs of mud onto the earth around it.

Gina ran towards it, her vision obscured by the dense smoke that enveloped her.

Ben bellowed a warning.

As she reached the edge of the pool, she turned. Her face was radiant. She thought she was safe. Her eyes sought his. He sprinted for her.

Dark smoke swept into the pool behind her. A wave of boiling mud rose up like a giant clawed hand. Its talons closed around her.

"No!" Ben screamed as Gina was pulled back towards the pool. She clawed at the ground, but its pull was relentless.

Her body splashed in and she was sucked down under the mud.

Ben reached the pool and dove down next to it. The heat was intense but he thrust his arms in, trying to catch her. He felt her fingers and pulled, tugging her, crying with pain as his flesh burned.

Her face emerged from the depths, her perfect skin scorched and blistered, mud clinging to her like a second skin.

A hideous gurgling came from her throat as she struggled to breathe.

"Ben," she whispered, and he saw the light go out in her eyes.

Her hand slipped from his as her body sank back into the depths.

Ben roared his pain to the sky as he knelt by the boiling pool. In the bubbling of the mud, he heard the dark laughter of Whiro as the god devoured another soul.

A cracking sound came from behind him. Ben turned as a geyser exploded from the earth and a blazing, toxic rain spilled from it. The fissure beyond opened up, wrenching apart the walls of the Institute. The boiling mud erupted into it, pouring into the gaps. The screams of those dying inside echoed to the sky.

Ben knelt in horror, watching his world end. He was nothing in the face of such destructive power. He beat his fists on the earth as tears streamed down his face. Everything was lost.

CHAPTER 25

RANGI HAD NEVER SEEN his grandmother react this way before.

Lucy started to pull the string over her head to give it to Aroha, but his grandmother put her hands out.

"No, no. It's yours. I feel it. No other can carry this."

Aroha stood and walked to Rangi. She leaned close.

"You were meant to meet this girl," she said as she clutched his hand with gnarled fingers. "As a young boy, you would sit here and take in all the stories of the gods. You would say the *karakia* prayers with a pure heart. They have not forgotten you, even though you were lost to us for many years." She nodded towards Lucy. "Protect her as she takes the *taonga* north to *Te Rerenga Wairua* – the leaping-off place where the spirits of the dead enter the under-world. That is what you were born to do."

Rangi bent and wrapped his big arms around his grandmother. Her frail body had a strength in it that seemed greater than his massive bulk.

"How do I know what to do?" he whispered. "I need your help."

Aroha pulled out of his embrace. She shook her head.

"No, boy. You don't need my help. Just listen to the wind, to the earth, to the pulse of your blood that beats with the heart of Aotearoa. You were named for Ranginui, god of the sky. This is your land." She looked over at Lucy. "This is her land, too. Only Maori and Pakeha together can appease the Risen Gods now."

A rumble came from deep within the earth.

The ground rippled. The walls of the meeting house shook.

Screams came from outside as a massive quake hit.

"Time is running out," Aroha said, her eyes wide. "You must go now, or the earth will soon mourn the passing of this land."

The quake intensified, shaking them to their knees. A mighty crack came from outside and screams filled the air.

A man ran inside, bracing himself against the pillars of the meeting house as he struggled to stay upright.

"There's been an eruption," he shouted. "Tongariro. It's blowing. Aroha, we need to get you out of here."

Rangi crawled to Lucy. She cradled Amber's head in her arms, sheltering her in case the building should crumble.

"We have to go, Lucy," Rangi said.

"I can't leave Amber," Lucy said. "I left her before and put her in danger."

Aroha came to kneel next to Amber and took the girl's pale hand in her own.

"Look at me, girl," she said to Lucy. Her voice was strong. Lucy obeyed, meeting the old woman's dark eyes. "Your sister is held captive by the same forces that now wreak havoc on the land. Her body is linked to your quest now." Aroha pointed at Lucy's pendant. "You are chosen to take the *taonga* north. When the land is saved, Amber will wake. If you refuse …" She shook her head. "Then hope is lost, and we have squandered our chance."

Tears ran down Lucy's face. "I didn't ask for this," she whispered.

Aroha chuckled. "Do you think the gods ask our permission?" She placed her hand on Amber's forehead, stroking the girl's brow. "I'll look after her, but your sister will grow weaker as the country suffers. She will die with it, unless you take up this quest. Go now or all is lost."

Lucy bent and kissed Amber's cheek.

"I'll be back," she whispered. She stood and turned to Rangi. "I'm ready."

* * *

They drove north again, back around the lake and into the forest. Every kilometer away from Amber made Lucy's heart sink further. Would she ever see her sister again? Was she doing the right thing? She clutched the pendant around her neck. Back in the *marae*, Aroha's words had seemed right and real. She believed in the quest. But now … What did she think she was doing?

As they emerged from the trees out onto the main road, Rangi gasped. Lucy looked up at the sound.

To the southwest, huge clouds billowed in hues of grey and black, belching from the volcano at Tongariro. They hung heavy in the sky, slow-moving but inexorably blowing over the land.

"Ruaumoko wakes," Rangi said. "We can't go back through Taupo. It'll be chaos."

He turned north towards Whakatane and

Tauranga. As they drove along the coast of the Bay of Plenty, Lucy looked out to the forbidding ocean. There was danger on all sides as the land she loved had turned against its people. She thought of Ben. Was he safe? Would she ever see him again?

CHAPTER 26

RAGE FLOWED THROUGH BEN as he knelt in the midst of destruction.

No more, he thought.

He would not let Gina die in vain, and he would honor Tamati's memory. He touched the talismans around his neck. He would get them north. For Grandfather. For Gina. For Lucy, if she was still out there. But now, he had to get out of town and back to the road.

He ran, away from the sirens and sounds of chaos. His muscles ached and he panted and gasped, but the physical movement anchored him. He was still alive. He ran until his rage ebbed and his grief dimmed a little.

He finally stopped on the edge of Whakarewarewa Forest. The sun cast lines of saffron light into the western sky, while bands of purple and blue crept into the east. Ben sat down to catch his breath, his back against a thick totara tree. Birdsong filtered through the trees. Despite the destruction, the world continued to turn. He closed his eyes and rested for a moment.

A rustle came from the trees behind him.

Ben remained still and silent. He didn't have the strength to fight anymore.

He heard a stomp followed by a soft whicker and opened his eyes. A brown horse with a black mane stepped from the shadows and walked towards him. Ben held his hand out, palm up.

"Here, boy," he said quietly.

The horse came closer and ducked its head into Ben's hand, encouraging him to give it a rub between the ears.

"Hey, buddy. Ever been to Auckland?"

His grandfather had taught him how to ride. The two had explored the woods and trails of the South Island when Ben was young. As he'd become older and more fascinated with horsepower over horses, Ben had lost interest. His grandfather believed that the animals had a deep connection to the earth goddess, Papatuanuku. Whatever the connection, Ben was glad of the companionship now. He stood and stroked the horse's flank. Its warmth comforted him.

He wrapped his hand into the thick mane and pulled himself onto the horse's back. It pranced a little, then relaxed.

"There, boy," he said, stroking it and willing himself to calm, knowing that the highly sensitive creature would pick up his emotions.

"North, then," he said after a minute. He gave the horse a little nudge with his heels and they trotted through the forest. Ben used the position of the sun to make sure they kept a northerly direction.

A little later, they emerged onto a ridge overlooking a shadowed valley. The horse stopped, stomping a little. It pawed at the ground.

Ben patted its neck as it whinnied.

"Something here you don't like. I get it," Ben said. "We'll be alright. C'mon."

He gave the horse a gentle nudge with his heel and they rode into the valley. A creek cut through the middle. The water ran northeast and wound through dense, old-growth trees.

Ben dismounted and the horse bent to drink from the creek. He dropped to his knees and splashed handfuls of water on his face, washing the ash and mud from his skin. Dark swirls formed in the water and tears pricked his eyes as he thought of Gina and Tamati, both taken by something he couldn't possibly triumph over. Ben clenched his fists. *No, he thought. There must be a way. I have to find it.*

The horse whinnied again and pawed at the ground, tossing its mane. Ben rose to calm it, but it reared up on its hind legs and kicked at the air. It turned and galloped east, away from the creek and out of the valley.

Something had spooked it.

Ben stood in stillness as the sound of its hoof-beats faded. Water gurgled over the rocks, but the forest was silent. Then, he heard a gurgle and a wet sucking sound that came from beneath the creek.

The bank shifted. Suddenly, a huge hole opened up. A gigantic reptilian head poked out, covered in slick, green scales. Its yellow eyes flickered towards Ben and the creature's forked tongue stabbed at the air. Ben froze as it emerged fully. It had to be seven feet long.

He remembered his grandfather's stories of the *taniwha*, the guardian of sacred places. The giant lizard opened its mouth and hissed, a dank sound of wet and dark places where the dead rotted under weeds and rocks. Tendrils of black smoke escaped with its breath.

Ben scrambled back from the creek's edge as the creature clawed its way towards him. Its tail thrashed behind, whipping the water into froth.

Ben turned and ran, stumbling through the rocky landscape, slipping on the wet stones. The *taniwha* was fast over its own terrain. Its footsteps slapped the ground, hissing only yards behind. Ben knew those claws would rake him to the bone if he fell. He dashed around trees and under low-hanging branches, the sour stench of rot coming closer.

His foot struck an embedded rock and he fell. The top half of his body hit the cold water and his knees scraped the bank. He rolled over. The *taniwha* was less than five yards away.

Ben scrambled to his feet and winced with the pain. The ligament of his left ankle sent a sharp pain up his leg. He pushed through it, climbing over the bank and back on to dry land as the *taniwha* snapped at his heels. He ran, searching his memory for anything that could help him. Then, he remembered a story his grandfather had told him long ago.

Ben turned away from the creek and clambered up the hill, towards the ridge where he had descended earlier. He pulled his way up the hillside, grabbing on to the exposed roots. The *taniwha* climbed after him, but its speed slowed uphill.

"C'mon, you ugly-ass lizard," he shouted. "Follow me."

As it climbed, the creature's scales turned from dark green to a light grey. It began to wheeze.

Ben turned and waited for the monster at the top

of the ridge. The creek was fifty yards below now, on the floor of the valley. He had remembered that the ancient guardian drew its energy from water – luring it away made the *taniwha* less powerful.

At least it gave him a chance.

Ben grabbed a dead branch from the forest floor. He swung it like a sword, getting a feel for the weight and reach.

The *taniwha* emerged from the incline. Ben swung the branch at the creature and struck it on the side of its head. There was a wet, popping sound and the *taniwha* hissed, clawing at him.

One of the sharp talons caught his arm, slashing it open. Bright blood spilled to the earth. The pain focused Ben, and he redoubled his efforts.

He darted to one side and lunged with one motion, the branch up behind his head, ready to strike. Before the *taniwha* could reach him, Ben slammed the branch down hard on the top of the creature's head. The *taniwha*'s skull cracked, and the branch snapped in half. Ben took a step back as the creature moaned, just a dying animal now.

It stumbled, its eyes focused on the creek below. But its home was too far away.

The creature's scales turned from grey to white. Its eyes dulled. It sank down to the leafy forest floor, collapsing as it died. Ben watched as the *taniwha*'s body shriveled, its scales burning into ash from an unseen flame. Tendrils of dark smoke dissipated into the air.

Ben sat down heavily, stilling his breathing as the sounds of the forest returned. The bubbling of water from the creek was peaceful again. His arm flamed with pain, his whole body ached, and all he wanted to do was lie down and rest on the cool moss of the forest floor.

But the talismans still tugged him north.

I've come too far, he thought. *I can't stop now.*

He pulled himself up against a tree and walked to the end of the ridge. Through the trees, he could see a road. He broke into a jog. The pain from his twisted ankle flared but Ben ran through it, determined now.

He pushed through the trees to where the road split the forest. It ran parallel with the creek, north to south. He scanned the trees for any sign of the horse, but his four-legged friend was nowhere to be seen.

Ben took a deep breath and hobbled north along the shoulder of the road. His mouth felt like cotton and his head ached. At least it took his focus from his swelling ankle and the gash in his arm.

The throbbing sound of an engine came from the south. He had to get to Auckland, and he wouldn't be able to get there on foot. He stuck out his thumb and turned to face the oncoming vehicle.

A battered red van turned the corner. An old woman sat behind the wheel, her silver hair tied into a bun on the top of her head. She pulled up next to Ben and wound down the window.

"Need a ride?" she asked.

"Yes, thanks for stopping." Ben got in, his nose wrinkling at the meaty smell inside.

The woman noticed his reaction. "Don't mind the smell, love. It's pet food. I was on a supply run for my pet store when this all happened. I sell reptiles."

"Great," said Ben. "Just great."

CHAPTER 27

LUCY AND RANGI FINALLY made it over the Bombay Hills and into Auckland late that afternoon. Even taking it in turns to drive, the long slow route in piles of traffic meant it took much longer than expected. The mundanity of traffic jams seemed to indicate all was well in the world, but the ash cloud from the south grew thicker, tendrils seeping to the edge of New Zealand's most densely populated area.

"We need to get further north," Rangi said. "This isn't over yet. There are those who believe that Auckland is well overdue for an eruption, and if Ruaumoko is woken ..."

His voice trailed off. He shook his head, his shoulders slumped. Lucy could hear exhaustion in his voice. She knew how he felt.

"We also need rest and food," she said. "My aunt

is in Takapuna, not too far off the road north. We could rest there before we push on."

Lucy drove them over the Harbor Bridge, glancing out across the city to the east and the Waitakere Range to the west. She and Ben had sailed here many times over the years, sometimes paired on racing yachts, other times competing separately on the Moths or other boats. They had both won their share of gold cups since they were children. They used to keep a tally, but Lucy couldn't even remember anymore who had won the most. Crazy to think they had once cared about such things.

She turned off the highway towards Takapuna Beach, but as they reached her aunt's road, Lucy continued straight on. She couldn't face talking about her parents' death or Amber's sickness. She didn't know what the hell was going on, but if she saw her aunt, she would crumble. She would weep for what she had lost and crawl into bed and curl up and sleep for days. And there was no time for that now.

"Are you OK?" Rangi asked, as Lucy pulled into a carpark on the edge of Takapuna Beach.

She got out of the car and walked over to the sea wall. The coastal wind was strong off the ocean and she pulled her fleece tighter around her. Rangi came to stand next to her and they both looked out towards Rangitoto Island, the perfect cone of the dormant volcano that sat in the Hauraki Gulf, the gateway to Auckland Harbor. The island was ringed with pohutukawa and rata trees, the deep green of the foliage standing out against the opal blue waters surrounding it. But beneath the waves, the creatures of the ocean waited. Lucy shuddered, thinking of the Strait crossing, the nightmare that had taken its fill of the dead.

A shadow passed overhead, the first clouds beginning to darken the sky.

Rangi looked up. "Looks like a storm's coming."

"What are we even doing here?" Lucy said. "I should be with Amber. That's why I couldn't stop at my aunt's place – I just don't know how to explain anything."

Rangi turned to her, his dark eyes kind. "I only know that for the first time in years, I have a purpose. To protect you and take you north. The gods will play their hand, but while I still have breath, I'll be with you."

His words made Lucy smile despite the turmoil inside. She had lost so much, but she had found an unlikely friend in this man.

The chill wind picked up even more. It grew darker as black clouds scudded across the sky.

"Ash from the south?" Lucy said, looking up.

"Maybe," Rangi replied. "But look out there."

The top of the island glowed in the rising darkness, a red halo above the ring of its cone that pulsed scarlet into the clouds above.

"Bloody sky," Rangi whispered. "It's the Maori name for the volcano. The *iwi* hold its eruption in tribal memory. They saw its destructive path six hundred years ago."

A deep rumble came from across the gulf. Lucy imagined molten rock rising within the volcano, pushing against the boulders that held the lava within.

"We need to go," Rangi said, reaching for her hand. "We can't help here. We can only take the *taonga* north."

* * *

Ben hopped out of the van at the edge of the Viaduct and thanked the old woman. He slammed the door shut and turned to face the harbor. Crowds of people down by the waterfront looked out towards Rangitoto Island. Even as the sky darkened above them, many filmed on their phones, faces alive with excitement. Others watched warily as they clutched the hands of their children. Above the wind, the sound of sirens split the air.

A red haze hovered over the volcano, sparks shooting up into the black clouds that squatted above it. Ben thought he saw creatures in the smoke, with fangs and wings like contaminated angels.

He turned to a spiky-haired teenager who leaned against a lamp post smoking a cigarette as if everything were still right in the world.

"What's going on?" Ben asked.

"Rangitoto. Shit's about to erupt. It's the end of the world, man."

Ben shook his head. If this was the 'big one,' Auckland would be smothered by tons of ash and the Risen Gods would win.

He couldn't let that happen.

The talismans pulsed against his skin and he felt that overwhelming need to go further north again. Perhaps there was still time.

Ben pushed through the throng of spectators into the back streets, deserted now as people hurried to watch, oblivious to the impending disaster. A motorcycle leaned against the wall, key still in the ignition, abandoned as the downtown area had filled with people. But now, the streets were almost empty and Ben was sure he could make it out of town.

He hopped on the bike, flipped the kickstand back, and pushed the ignition button. The BMW motorcycle started up and Ben gunned the throttle while kicking it down into first gear. He glanced into the side mirror as he rode down Quay Street, catching a glimpse of the ash cloud as its shadow moved across the harbor towards the crowd.

CHAPTER 28

AS THE SUN SET, Ben rested the motorcycle against the gate to Waipoua Forest. He needed to stop for a rest and he was drawn to this spot by the memory of visiting the ancient tree here years ago. Tane Mahuta, Lord of the Forest. He could use some of that ancient wisdom now.

There was dust and ash in the air and Ben could taste sulfuric grit in his mouth despite wearing a bandana over his face during the ride. *What I would give for a beer right now.* Ben smiled at the thought.

The motorcycle's hot engine pinged as it cooled. He was careful not to let his leg touch the exhaust pipes as he dismounted on shaky legs. The ride north had been challenging. Some people helped others at times of crisis, but some saw chaos as a dark opportunity. Ben had seen both on the road, but he didn't stop. Time was running out now. He felt an urgency spill from the talismans that rested on his chest.

He stood on the edge of the forest and let his eyes adjust to the dark. Kauri trees towered above and the smell of rain on ferns hung in the air. He breathed the cool air deep into his lungs.

A branch snapped nearby.

Ben started. He held his breath and waited, listening intently.

Nothing.

He scanned the forest around him. The black shapes looming above him seemed less welcoming now. He didn't have a flashlight, yet he still felt drawn onward. Tane Mahuta was further in, and you did not ignore the Lord of the Forest.

Ben took two steps down the trail and then looked back over his shoulder at the motorcycle. All he had to do was jump on it and ride away. He could find somewhere to hide out from this madness. After all, could he really have any impact on what was happening to the country?

He shook his head. It seemed like a crazy quest, but he had come too far to stop now.

He carried on down the trail.

The low-hanging branches reached for him, thin skeleton arms snagging his shirt. A spider web, invisible in the dark, wrapped around his face. Ben's heart pounded as he swatted at the darkness, ripping the sticky threads from his skin. He imagined the smoke of Whiro winding its way through the forest after him, the talons of the demon reaching out to rip his flesh from his bones.

Stop it, Ben thought. He pushed away the image of his grandfather's death. It wouldn't help him now.

He followed the footpath through the forest until he reached the great Lord of the Forest himself, Tane Mahuta. Ben put his hand against the trunk, feeling the rough bark under his palm.

There was no beating heart, but this great kauri tree was thought to be over two thousand years old. It had stood here, quiet in the forest, as the great empires of the world rose and fell. Most of the Northland kauri trees had been felled over the years, but this one remained among a few of its kin. The trunk was so wide that twelve people could stand around its girth with arms outstretched and still not touch each other's fingers.

Ben leaned forward, rested his forehead against the bark and closed his eyes. He felt powerless and insignificant standing beneath the ancient tree and strangely, that was comforting. The giant kauri had grown here as generations of people were born and died. It would outlive whatever came to pass in the days to come. Not that he knew what that would be.

He felt for the talismans around his neck. They had become lighter as he traveled north and now it seemed as if they rested, waiting for something. *Why am I here?*

There was another crack in the darkness, back along the path. Ben turned from the kauri.

"Who's there?" he called.

Then, the trees around him shivered as a huge figure emerged from the dark.

It barreled into him.

Ben went down hard, air rushing from his lungs. In the dark, he saw black hair and fierce teeth. A fist raised, about to crash down into his face.

"Ben?"

The voice was soft, hesitant. He recognized it immediately.

"Lucy?"

"It's alright, Rangi. He's a friend."

Rangi climbed off Ben, and then Lucy was there. In his arms at last. They clung to each other.

"I thought –"

"Are you –"

Their words tumbled over one another, both of them laughing as they embraced. Rangi stood watch over them as they caught up quickly on what had happened to them both after the tidal wave. It seemed incredible that they had both made it this far.

"As we drove north, I felt drawn here somehow," Lucy said. "That's how we found you."

She pulled her pendant out and Ben tugged his own from under his shirt.

Rangi shone a torch down onto them as they examined the talismans. He reached out a finger as if to touch them, his eyes curious, and then he pulled away.

"Do you – feel – anything when they touch your skin?" Lucy's voice was hesitant, and Ben understood how she felt.

"Yeah, weird, eh."

They both laughed softly.

"Now I feel a tug north again," Lucy said.

"I wonder how far we have to go." Ben tucked the talismans back into his shirt.

"All the way to *Te Rerenga Wairua*, Cape Reinga." Rangi's voice was solemn and deep. "The leaping-off place where the spirits of the dead enter the underworld. My grandmother told me to take you there, Lucy."

"She's a *kaumatua*," Lucy explained to Ben. "She's helping Amber, and I trust her word."

"It's further north," Ben said, "so that makes sense. If we go now, we can make it within a few hours."

"You're not going anywhere."

The voice came from the darkness in the trees

around them. The three of them spun around, looking for the source.

A man stepped out of the shadows, a serrated knife in one hand.

Rangi started towards the man but five more figures emerged from the darkened forest, guns at the ready. They were dressed in pig-hunting gear, rifles held easy in their hands. Rangi stepped back, hands raised.

"It's OK, man," he said. "We're moving on. Not looking for any trouble."

The leader turned his torch on, shining it up under his chin. The light caught the edges of two ugly wounds on his cheeks, the slashes turning his visage into a nightmare.

"Too late," he said. "You brought this trouble upon yourself."

CHAPTER 29

LUCY GASPED AS THE man's face was revealed. Rangi's fists tightened, and one of the men shoved a gun into his back.

"What's going on?" Ben asked. "What trouble?"

Sitona grabbed Lucy's wrist and pulled her forward, spinning her around. He curled one arm about her neck and held the knife against her cheek in the same place as his own wounds. Ben saw wisps of black smoke curling around the man's clothes. *Whiro*.

"Tell him, pretty one," Sitona said.

"He had Amber," Lucy stumbled over the words. "He was taking children."

"Merchandise that you stole from me," Sitona spat in her ear. He tucked his knife away and reached around to cup her breast. "But you'll make up for your sister, at least." He squeezed her breast hard and Lucy whimpered, her face frozen in fear.

"Leave her alone." Rangi rushed forward, trying to get to her.

One of the hunters stepped forward and slammed the butt of his gun into Rangi's middle. As Rangi bent in pain, the hunter whipped it round and jabbed it at the big man's face. There was a crunch and Rangi fell to his knees, hands to his nose as blood gushed from the wound.

Sitona laughed.

"You're gonna have to do better than that. It's hunting season and I promised these guys an animal to practice on."

Ben heard the dark promise in the man's words even as he assessed the rough men around them, looking for possible escape. Pig hunting was sport up here, with dogs and knives and guns. It wouldn't have cost much to get these guys onside, and they would relish a fight. With Rangi injured, there was no way out. Not yet.

"Let's get them back to the camp," Sitona said, shoving Lucy in front of him.

One of the hunters jabbed Ben in the ribs with his gun, forcing him onto another track that wound away from the giant kauris and off the marked trail.

As they walked, torches flickered from the men in front and behind. The night felt heavy on Ben's shoulders, as if the evil seeping through the forest would prevent the sun from rising. As the hunters marched them deeper into the forest, Ben felt the calm peace of Tane Mahuta's kingdom recede. In its place, Whiro's presence surged.

Lucy walked in front of him and Rangi behind. Ben could hear the big man wheezing, his nose bloody from the beating. Lucy tripped on a trailing root. One of the men grabbed her by the elbow and yanked upward. She cried out, stifling the sound as the man pulled her towards him, taking the chance to touch her skin.

"Where are you taking us?" Ben asked, trying to draw attention away from her.

A gun barrel cracked into his ribs. He bent in pain and a meaty hand slammed down on the back of his head. Ben's vision exploded with stars.

"Keep walking, boy."

The silent, dark forest swirled about them, then Ben saw lights ahead. They came to a clearing in the forest lit by the orange flicker of a campfire, with two more men sitting next to it. One turned a spit and the other pulled a crate of beer towards him. Dogs ran out from the fireside, barking and growling as they bared their teeth at the strangers. Ben had seen pig-dogs like these tear animals apart, snarling at the kill. He stepped warily around them.

The smell of roast pork wafted over from the

fire as chunks of meat charred in the flames. Ben's mouth watered and his belly rumbled. But under the rich scent was the smell of butchered animals and blood.

Two cocoon shapes hung from branches at the perimeter of the camp, wild pig carcasses from the day's hunting. The dogs turned away from the strangers to nose at a pile of entrails under the carrion. The wind pushed the meat back and forth, the pigs' eyes staring out into the dark.

"We eat now, play after," the biggest hunter said with a tone of authority.

Sitona nodded. "But tie them up first. And tie that one up good." He nodded towards Rangi.

The hunter pulled Lucy towards him, running his hands over her buttocks. "I'll tie this one up."

"Careful," Sitona said. "She's merchandise now."

The hunter pushed his face close to Sitona's. "I won't mark 'er but I *will* have 'er."

Ben saw the lust in the man's eyes and heard a growl from Rangi's throat. They would not last long here.

The hunters pushed them down under the carrion tree and tied their wrists with rough rope, the same used to hang their kill. Sitona watched as they wrapped cords around Ben and Rangi's feet, hobbling them. The big hunter leered at Lucy.

"I'll leave your legs free, darlin'. Easy access for later." He laughed as his hungry eyes raked over her bound body. She cowered under his gaze.

"Let her go," Ben said. "Keep us here, but let her go, please."

The man grunted. "My door don't swing that way. And me and my boys gonna have some fun tonight. Maybe you two can even watch." He hefted the knife at his side. "Then we'll have some hunting practice with you animals."

He hawked and spat, the stinking spittle dripping off Ben's chin as he walked back to the campfire to drink. Sitona followed, glancing back to check his merchandise was safe before he nodded and accepted a beer. The clink of bottles soon filled the air and the men began to feast on the roasted meat.

"Are you alright?" Ben whispered.

"Fine." Lucy was curt. She turned to Rangi. "Are you hurt?" she asked the big Maori.

"Not enough," Rangi said, his voice sharp even with the broken nose. "They'll pay for this."

Ben grinned. He was glad to have Rangi on their side.

"My rope isn't very tight," Lucy whispered. "They didn't want to mark me so I think I can slide my hands out."

"Careful," Rangi whispered back. "Go slowly."

Lucy wriggled a little, working at the bonds that held her. One of the dogs looked up from the carcass. It snarled and then turned its attention back to the intestines.

Ben saw the rope drop away and Lucy shuffled slowly over to Rangi. Ben kept an eye on the campfire. The men shared jokes, laughing and drinking. One man stood to take a piss and collapsed in a drunken heap. Two of the others jumped up and proceeded to kick him in the ribs, high-fiving each other and taking more swigs from the bottles. Smoke from the fire obscured them, but Ben thought he saw their faces contorted into empty skulls as the black mist swirled about them.

Then Lucy was behind him, working at the knots with her slim fingers.

A minute later, Ben felt the pressure on his wrists release and he used his right hand to massage his left wrist, then did the other.

"We need to hurry," he whispered. "They're almost done."

"Across from the fire. There." Rangi nodded his head in the direction of three Jeeps parked side by side.

"The dogs?"

Rangi looked over his shoulder. A couple of them were still gorging themselves on pig entrails and two others lay asleep, sated from the feast.

"We can make it." Rangi nodded at them both. "You ready?"

Ben and Lucy nodded. This was their only chance. Ben took one last look at the campfire. The pig hunters were drunk, but these were hard men. The three of them could probably get to the Jeep. But after that, he wasn't sure. Whiro didn't give up.

"Go," Rangi said.

Lucy jumped up and ran. Ben stood quickly, but his legs felt soft and weak. Rangi grabbed him by the arm, hauling him forward.

The dogs barked, racing after them.

Shouts and the sounds of bottles breaking came from the campfire.

"Get them!"

Ben turned to see the silhouette of the big hunter running towards them. His knife gleamed in the firelight. Sitona raced after him, the other men behind.

Ben jumped into the driver's seat. The keys dangled from the ignition. Northlanders didn't worry about having their vehicles stolen this deep in the forest.

"Go," Lucy said, her voice strong in Ben's ear.

He stomped on the clutch, turned the key, and gunned the accelerator. The engine came alive and Ben dropped the Jeep into first gear while slamming the gas pedal to the floor.

The rear tires spun, throwing dirt and rocks into the faces of the pig hunters, buying Ben a few more precious seconds. He grabbed the headlamp switch and the beams illuminated a two-lane dirt road. The rear tires finally caught, and the Jeep fishtailed back and forth across the road before picking up speed.

Behind them, Sitona and the hunters jumped into two other vehicles and roared after them.

CHAPTER 30

B EN SHIFTED GEARS, SPEEDING along the track.

"They're coming," Rangi said, his hands clutching the roll bars as he looked out the back.

Ben glanced into the rearview mirror. Headlights bobbed behind them as the Jeep bounced along the track through the bush.

"Turn here!" Rangi shouted.

They skidded out of the bush and onto Ninety Mile Beach, sand spraying out from beneath the wheels.

Ben yanked the wheel hard and pressed the accelerator down. They zoomed onto the flat of the sand and pulled away as the two other Jeeps emerged from the bush, one of them jumping a dune to land a few meters away.

Lucy turned to see the frenzied faces of the men

in the Jeeps. Their eyes were crazed and feral, like they were possessed by something beyond this world.

They hooted like animals and bared their teeth, screaming for blood – a pack of predators closing in. They were all just animals now.

"Faster!" Rangi shouted.

He climbed into the back of the Jeep, pushing Lucy forward towards Ben on the front seat. He picked up a wrench and hung out the back of the vehicle, cursing at the men in *Te Reo*.

"Can we outrun them?" Lucy said.

"We're going to try." Ben clenched his teeth as he shifted gears and zigzagged towards the surf. The sun glinted on the water. Out west, Lucy thought she saw the huge curve of a monster's tail and the dark undertow of giant creatures. The water wasn't safe, but neither was the land. They were trapped.

Sitona drove one of the Jeeps closer and rammed them hard.

Ben struggled to maintain control of the vehicle. The front wheels touched the water, slowing them down. He swerved inland again.

One of the men jumped over the gap between the vehicles, his hands grabbing the roll bar.

He barreled into Rangi in the back. The two men went down, clutching at each other.

The feral man scratched and bit, but Rangi was faster. He smashed the wrench into the other man's face.

Lucy heard the crunch of bone and bright blood spurted out. Rangi hit him again and the man slumped on the floor of the Jeep.

The big Maori picked up the man's body and hurled it at the vehicle in pursuit. They ran it over, barely stopping, laughing and hooting. Lucy looked over and one thrust his crotch at her.

"Won't be long, pretty," he shouted, his words whipped away by the wind.

Rangi panted with exertion, and Lucy could see how tired he was. He couldn't hold them off by himself, and there was nothing in front of them but miles of beach.

"Fuel's low," Ben said. "We can't keep on like this."

Then, the two 4WDs pulled alongside.

The ferals slammed into the car from the side, the metallic clash ringing out over the noise of the surf. Ben dipped in and out of the waves, fighting to keep control.

The Jeep bucked when it hit a rock.

Ben lost control and they skidded across the slick sand. The Jeep tipped over, spilling the three of them into the waves, tumbling over each other as they came to a rest in the shallow surf.

Lucy landed heavily, pain shooting up her arm as it broke her fall. The cold of the water made her gasp, and she struggled out from beneath the side of the Jeep, aware that the men were only meters away. The rev of their engines came to a stop, and the thump of their feet landing on the sand made her look round in despair.

Ben lay with his eyes closed in the shallow water, a deep cut on his head oozing blood that swirled in the bubbles of the surf. Lucy went to him and pulled him into a sitting position.

"Come on, Ben," she said in desperation. "I need you. We have to move."

He groaned and opened his eyes slightly, but she knew he needed time to recover.

Rangi stumbled to his feet, standing in front of Ben and Lucy as the men approached. There were five of them, each with eyes wide and bloodshot.

The biggest hunter hefted a tire iron in his hands. Sitona held a baseball bat, while yet another man grabbed the metal wrench from the sand, where it had fallen from the truck. Their eyes narrowed as they studied their prey.

Rangi spread his arms wide, standing tall, his bulk a formidable barrier.

"You wanna play, monkey man," the big hunter sneered. "Won't take long." His eyes darted to Lucy and he licked his lips at the wet clothes that clung to her body. "Then we'll have some real fun."

Rangi charged, his speed surprising. His thick arm caught the hunter around his neck and clotheslined him to the sand. Rangi roared as he hit the feral with full force.

The other men closed in, swinging their bats and weapons. There were four of them now.

"No!" Lucy cried out as her friend was overwhelmed by the force of them.

He broke out of their attack, shouting curses as he swung at the men. A deep warrior cry broke from his chest, a primal sound that reverberated through Lucy's body and made the hair on her arms stand on end.

Two of the feral men went down from his powerful blows, his teeth bared as he struck at their flesh.

Lucy crouched under the shadow of the Jeep. It was as if she saw an ancient tribal battle before her. Rangi was a great warrior sent to protect them, a man of legend, a man of whom tales would be told. But his face was covered in blood, and she wanted to weep as he tired.

She heard the words of Aroha, his grandmother, in her head. This was Rangi's fate. He was sent for this, and he met it willingly.

Sitona broke through and landed a powerful blow to the back of Rangi's head.

The big man fell to his knees, his shoulders bent as he struggled to shake off the pain. His eyes glazed over. He looked to Lucy, his face stricken, his dark eyes desolate at his failure to protect them.

Sitona moved to the side, raising the tire iron, its wicked hook end about to crash down into Rangi's skull.

Another man stabbed a knife towards the big Maori's neck.

Lucy saw it happen in slow motion and she started running to her friend, to the man who had saved her sister.

"Rangi," she screamed, her feet flashing across the shining sand, trying desperately to get to him, to stop the men.

Sitona looked up and laughed, swinging the tire iron down as the hunter drove the knife into Rangi's neck. There was a crunch of metal against bone and Rangi fell face down, his blood soaking the golden sand.

Lucy screamed, wailing to the sky as she reached her friend. She sank down to her knees and grasped the pendant around her neck, her rage exploding at the men who circled her now, their faces fixed on her body with hungry eyes.

She called on Papatuanuku, goddess of the earth, whose flesh was stone and rock and sand and mud.

Goddess of this land, of this Aotearoa.

The beach rippled around the men, rising up like a wave. Lucy grabbed fistfuls of the bloody sand and threw it in the air as she screamed her rage.

Sitona and the hunters turned in horror as the sand swirled about them, blinding them, slicing at their flesh.

They tried to run back to the Jeep, but the bloody sand opened up in a huge maw with ragged teeth of shell and stone. It swallowed them whole, their screams smothered as it covered their bodies and they were gone.

In a moment, all was quiet.

Seagulls called overhead and the surf swooshed on the sand. The dawn was breaking. But on the horizon, a line of black rose, the beginnings of a storm across the sea.

Lucy sobbed as she rolled Rangi over and pulled his bloody head onto her lap. She stroked his face. He still had a faint pulse, but his head wound was deep.

"Rangi," she whispered.

His eyes fluttered open. They were bloodshot and pained, but Lucy saw a glimmer of the man still inside.

"You and Ben must go," he whispered. "*Te Rerenga Wairua.*" He coughed, his throat gurgling with blood. "My spirit will race you there."

His eyes closed and he breathed for the last time. Lucy wept as she rocked him in her arms. She felt his spirit lighten and go back to join his ancestors.

Rangi Anahera was gone.

"I'll come back for you," Lucy whispered. "I'll make sure it's the best *tangi* your *marae* has ever seen."

A shadow fell across her and Lucy shivered, suddenly aware of the cold. She looked up to see clouds gathering above, whirling together in a vortex. She had seen this before, at the Strait crossing. Tawhirimatea, the god of storms, was no friend of theirs.

There were things up there in the clouds, too, wheeling and diving in the silver lightning that sparked across the black. Whatever they were, they were huge.

Lucy got to her feet as rain began to fall, drops so big they dented the sand. She ran back to the overturned Jeep. Ben was still woozy, but he was able to stand with Lucy's help.

"What happened?" he asked. "Rangi?"

"He's gone," Lucy said, her voice steel-hard now. "And we have to finish this."

They ran together for the feral men's Jeep as the rain lashed the beach and whipped the waves up into peaks. The wind howled as it buffeted them, the screams of the damned in the high-pitched noise. Ben stumbled, but Lucy pulled him onwards.

The Jeep was half-buried in sand, the engine covered in the stuff from where it had swallowed the feral men. There was no way it would start, even if they could dig it out.

The rain hammered at them now, soaking them both to the bone. The cold wind blew and they shivered uncontrollably. But the cold cleared Ben's head and he grabbed Lucy's hand, pulling her through the clinging sand towards the dunes. At least they could shelter there.

A cry broke the air, a shriek that seemed to split the sky.

* * *

Ben turned at the noise, looking up in horror as a gigantic bird dive-bombed them, its beak spear-sharp.

He pushed Lucy to the sand and dove down himself as the beak pierced the air where they had stood moments before. The bird swooped away and up again, preparing for another pass.

It cried into the storm, calling for its flock.

Ben rolled onto his back to look up, shielding his eyes against the rain as he focused on the giant birds of prey wheeling above.

They had alternating feathers as black as pitch and red as blood, tinged with the white of bone along the ends. Their wingspan stretched a full two meters across.

"*Hokioi*," Ben whispered, his heart pounding as he realized what they were.

Birds of myth belonging to the god of the winds, their presence a warning of war. Unearthly creatures set on stopping them from reaching Cape Reinga. Their beaks could pierce skin and bone and tear their limbs apart, before casting their bloody corpses upon the water.

But there was nowhere to go.

Ninety Mile Beach was a wilderness of sand and ocean. It would end here. They had failed.

The birds began to wheel together, the flock of giants beginning a pattern in the sky that seemed to feed off the lightning that sparked between them.

Then, with a great cry, they turned and pulled their wings in, dropping from the sky as one to dive-bomb the two humans who lay exposed on the ground beneath.

CHAPTER 31

AS THE BIRDS DOVE, hoofbeats pounded the ground, thudding through Ben.

He turned his head and there, from the grassy dunes, two wild horses galloped towards them. Their tawny manes flew in the wind, their hooves flying across the sand, their eyes narrowed against the stinging rain.

"Creatures of the land," Lucy whispered. "From Papatuanuku."

The horses galloped in circles around Ben and Lucy, standing between the humans and the birds. The giant *hokioi* screeched as they descended but they veered at the last minute, winging away from the horses, unable to wound creatures sent by the goddess.

The birds flew back into the stormy sky, wheeling overhead, beady eyes fixed on the humans below.

Ben watched them for a minute, wary of standing and attracting attention, but it seemed they would remain high up – at least for now.

The clouds grew thicker above them, shades of bruised purple slashed with silver forked lightning. Out to sea, a thick bank of cloud rolled towards them. Even from this far out, Ben could see shapes moving within it.

The horses nickered and nuzzled at Ben, pawing the sand as if eager to move on.

"They'll take us to the cape," Ben said, sure that they could make it. The call of the north was almost desperate inside him now, and he knew Lucy felt it too. "We can still get there."

Lucy leaned close to one horse, gathering a handful of its mane.

"Shh, it's alright," she whispered to it, stroking its flank. Then she turned to Ben. "Give me a boost."

Ben cupped his hand and she stepped up, mounting the horse to sit bareback. He looked up at her as the wind blew her blonde hair about her face. Against the darkening black of the sky, she was a golden statue, a representation of the goddess. He caught a glimpse of the pendant about her neck, a twin to his own shard of power. Together they would end this, or at least they would see the end of the country together.

A roll of thunder crashed over the sea, vibrating through the air. The horses neighed, pawing the sand with hooves raised. They needed to go.

Ben mounted the other horse, tugging its mane until it turned so they pointed north. He looked over at Lucy and she smiled. There was a wildness in her that matched his own. They were creatures of the land as much as the horses. They were embodied spirits, here to live and die in violence. If the land were to sink into the sea today, they would at least have seen some great adventures.

Lucy kicked her heels, and her horse set off up the beach as she bent low to its mane. Her delighted laughter rang out and Ben spurred his own mount on after her.

They raced down the beach, flying over the sand. Ben felt the heat of the horse beneath him, felt his own spirit soar, entwined with the creature whose hooves beat the earth as they dashed north. There was a moment when exhilaration overtook Ben and he tipped his head up to the sky. Rain lashed down on his face, and he understood how it was all linked together. How the balance had shifted, because the people had lost touch with the land and the creatures on it.

But in this moment, they were one again.

He let go of striving, let go of his grief for

Grandfather, for Gina, for Aotearoa. The gods would survive this, the earth would renew itself, even if humans were gone. Ben felt for the shard around his neck and sent out a prayer to the Risen Gods.

Forgive us.

Forgive me.

As if connected to his energy, the horse surged forward, hooves flashing beneath them. For a moment, Ben rode neck and neck with Lucy, and he reached out his hand. She looked over and reached for him in return. Their fingers touched, their eyes met, and the four creatures of the earth rode hard for the end of Ninety Mile Beach and onwards towards Cape Reinga.

Behind them, the storm gathered strength.

* * *

Finally, they reached the end of the road at Cape Reinga, known to the Maori as *Te Rerenga Wairua*, the leaping-off place where the spirits enter the underworld. The horses came to a halt in front of the deserted lighthouse. Their heads drooped with exhaustion and their flanks dripped from sweat and rain.

Lucy dismounted and leaned into her horse's neck, her forehead against him.

"Thank you," she whispered.

The horse whinnied gently and then stepped away from her. It nodded its head and then turned away, trotting south again. Ben came to stand next to her as his horse followed, and soon they were left alone at the tip of Aotearoa.

They stood on the clifftop looking north. There was a further short spit of land and then the ocean stretched into the distance, the next stop Noumea and the Pacific Islands.

The rain lashed down, but they could still see the boiling of the ocean where the Tasman Sea met the Pacific, two powerful streams meeting here. The energy from the waves rolled off the sea and white waters lashed the rocky shoreline. Lucy felt a tug towards the deep.

"We need to go further," she said, reaching for Ben's hand. "Out there."

"It's crazy," Ben said, shaking his head, but she knew he understood. Something called to them out there.

They walked away from the paved area, climbed outside the safety barriers, and clambered over the rocks towards the very end of the spit.

The storm was almost upon them now. The crash of lightning followed almost immediately by the roll of thunder vibrated through Lucy's chest – the anger of the gods that they would even dare try and prevent the end of this land.

Lucy slipped on a rock and fell hard to her knees, her hand scraping down a sharp rock as she tried to stop herself falling. Blood welled quickly and tears sprang to her eyes. She shivered under the onslaught of the rain. As she looked out at the boiling sea, Lucy suddenly felt desolate and empty. *What were they even doing here?*

Ben scrambled back up to help her.

"Are you alright?" he said.

"Crazy question." Lucy couldn't help but smile through her tears. "I don't think any of this is alright. Perhaps we're deluded in thinking that we can even stop this. That we can make a difference."

Ben pulled her into his arms and she relished his warmth. The rain slammed into them both, huddled on the rocks at the end of the country, perhaps at the end of it all.

"We're almost there," he whispered. "You and me. We've been through so much. We've lost so much. But we're together now, and I believe we're meant to be here."

He pulled away slightly, looking down into her eyes. In his dark gaze, Lucy could see that he was a different man now. Different from the Ben she had sailed with not so long ago. This man knew what lay beyond the physical realm. This man would fight the Risen Gods for his land.

For their land.

And she would fight with him.

"Together, then," she said, and he nodded.

Lucy pushed herself up from the rocks, forced away the pain in her bloody hand, ignored the icy wind that buffeted them. Ben led the way and they carefully climbed between the rocks to the very end of the cape.

There, lashed to a rock, was a wooden *waka* – a canoe with two paddles inside.

* * *

For a moment, Ben couldn't believe what he was seeing – although why he doubted after everything else that had happened in the last days, he wasn't sure. The *waka* was beautiful, carved from a single totara tree trunk and decorated with the faces of warriors and the stories of the gods, the motifs of his people. Legends told of the great *waka* that had come from *Hawaiki*, the mythical homeland.

The craft could take them further. He looked out at the churning surf and the clash of the two oceans. If they could make it out that far, of course.

A gigantic wave broke over the rocks. It soaked

Ben and Lucy and rocked the *waka* back against the craggy promontory. Ben clawed his way to it, laying a hand upon the wood. He felt a surge of power up his arm, jolting him and making his heart pound. The wood was alive with the power of the trees, of Tane Mahuta, of Papatuanuku. It was of the earth, and the waters would part for it.

Another wave crashed over them, and Ben lost his grip on the *waka*. The sense of power disappeared. They would be safe in the boat, but would they be able to stay in it? He turned to Lucy. She clung to the side of the *waka*, face pale with cold, her hands bloody, but her blue eyes were steel as she looked at him. She nodded.

It was time.

Together, they hauled the *waka* to the very edge of the ocean and stood in the face of the storm, waiting for a break in the waves.

Ben saw their chance and they pushed the *waka* forward into the surf. Lucy jumped in the front and paddled hard. Ben leapt in behind her. The stern crunched against the rocks and for a moment he thought they would be tipped out, rolled under the crashing waves. Then they surged out, surfing on the back of a reflected wave into the deep.

Ben whooped as they crested. For a moment, they could see the wide ocean before them. Lucy turned and laughed, her eyes bright, the momentary triumph overtaking them both.

Then her eyes widened as she looked up and past Ben.

"Oh no." He saw her mouth shape the words, but the sound was lost on the wind.

Ben turned, and saw their end in the approaching storm.

CHAPTER 32

BLACK CLOUDS TWISTED INTO a tornado of lightning and whirling smoke, as if the sky itself burned. Inside, creatures of fire and wind clawed towards them, talons of flame and soot reaching down towards the tiny *waka* on the waves that boiled beneath them.

Lucy smelled burning flesh on the air. In the clouds, she saw a vision of the great cities of New Zealand buried under the flow of red-hot lava as the gods took their fill of human sacrifice. Screams of the tortured and dying rang through the air, and she saw her parents die again and again in the destruction. Amber writhed in pain as the spirits took what was left of her.

"No," Lucy howled. She cowered and blocked her ears, closing her eyes against the horror.

Then Ben was there. His arms around her. His mouth close to her ear.

"It's not real," he said, squeezing her tight. "They want to stop us. But I need you to paddle, Lucy. We need to get away from the rocks or we will die here."

He shook her until she opened her eyes. Lucy focused on his strong gaze, trying to block out the gathering storm above.

"For Rangi," Ben said. "For Amber."

Lucy felt a surge of resolve and nodded. Rangi wouldn't give up. He would fight to the end. And she had to keep going for Amber's sake. It was her sister's only chance.

She took hold of the paddle again and together they plunged into the wild ocean, spray soaking them as they paddled harder, inch by inch towards the meeting of the oceans.

"There!" Ben shouted above the wail of the wind, pointing with his paddle.

As they rode the crest of a wave, Lucy saw it: a giant vortex in the ocean, a whirling mass of water that summoned all to its center, where it crushed everything down to the deep.

And it was pulling them closer by the second.

Creatures of the sea leapt as they tried to escape the powerful rip. Silver-grey flashes of huge sharks. Sharp spikes and purple sails of marlin and sailfish. All of them pulled in, inexorably downwards.

Then, a huge fleshy tentacle emerged from the

wave, hooked suckers clawing towards them as the giant eye of the mighty octopus fixed on its prey.

Lucy's heart thumped hard in her chest. There was no way they could escape this.

But then she felt the pull of the pendant – towards the center of the vortex.

She lifted her paddle and rested it in the *waka*. There was no need to paddle anymore. They were caught in the whirling waters, and it would draw them in and down where they were meant to be.

She thought of Amber and sent her love across the waves, hoping that somehow her sister would hear. Then she turned to Ben, scrambling over the seat to his open arms.

* * *

Ben held Lucy close as they spiraled towards the center of the vortex. His breath came fast in anticipation of what the end would feel like. But this time, he would hold onto her. They would go under together.

Offer the pendants now.

The deep voice came from within, but it was strong and powerful. Lucy leaned away from him, and Ben could see that she had heard it too.

The voice of Papatuanuku, goddess of the earth.

They both pulled the pendants from around their necks. Hers was the *manaia*, the messenger of the gods of the air. His was Te Wheke, the creature of the deep, entwined with the shard of the great *waka*.

Together, they bound land and sea. Together they represented Maori and Pakeha, male and female.

Hands entwined, Ben and Lucy waited until the *waka* rode the very edge of the vortex. Until they felt the vertigo of looking down into the center of the ocean.

They threw the pendants out into the waters, then watched as the *taonga*, the treasures of the people of the land, sank into the midnight blue.

As the pendants disappeared beneath the sea, the wind struck even more powerfully, whipping them around as the black clouds descended. Ben felt the roar of Whiro in the gale, the anger of the god against those who would challenge his dominance.

A huge wave struck the *waka,* and the pair were thrown to the floor. Water poured into the canoe, and they spun out of control. Ben grabbed for the paddle and tried to keep them upright. Lucy clung to the seat, her head buried against him.

Then, a plume of foam erupted from the center of the vortex. A jet of water shot upwards and pierced the black clouds swirling about them.

A deep rumble of thunder came from the land, an echoing groan from the deep ocean.

The wind receded. The clouds cleared. The waters calmed.

Ben and Lucy sat in the *waka* on a becalmed sea as a rainbow appeared in the sky. The treaty of the gods renewed.

"We made it," Lucy whispered.

Ben pulled her into his arms. Together, they watched an albatross circle above them, its call a promise of a new day.

CHAPTER 33

Two weeks later.

BEN HEFTED THE SAIL onto its rack, and then stood back to admire how the boathouse looked. The outside was still smashed up and this rack was only the beginning, but it was just one way that Christchurch was starting to recover.

The city would make it. Hell, the country would make it, because everyone was doing their bit in the aftermath of the disaster. The volcanic eruptions had calmed along with the ocean and it seemed that equilibrium had finally returned.

With a bit of number 8 wire, she'll be right, Ben thought with a smile at the Kiwi can-do attitude.

"What do you think of this?"

Lucy's voice came from the front of the boathouse and Ben walked back out into the sun to find her.

She held a paintbrush, her head tilted to one side as she examined the new sign for the Pegasus Bay Sailing Club. Amber sat on the grass next to her sister, staring out to sea. She was recovering slowly, but her cheeks had a touch of pink today and her eyes were brighter.

Ben looked at the sign. The fresh green paint glistened in the morning light. Under the name, Lucy had painted a *koru*, the unfurling frond of the silver fern. It was a Maori symbol of creation and new life, of perpetual movement and change in the lifecycle of the earth.

"Not bad," Ben said. "Might get you carving for the *marae* next. Maybe we can take something up for Rangi's *tangihanga*."

Lucy smiled softly and tears sprang to her eyes. They had all lost so much.

Ben wrapped his arms around her and leaned down to kiss her. He would take every moment to be close to Lucy now. Their shared memories of what they had seen would bind them together, whatever happened in the future. At least today, they had each other.

ENJOYED RISEN GODS?

If you enjoyed the book, we'd really appreciate a review on the site where you bought it. Your help in spreading the word is gratefully appreciated and reviews make a huge difference to helping new readers find the series. Thank you!

**You can get free books from the authors
by signing up below:**

Get a free dark fantasy trilogy from J. Thorn:
http://bit.ly/risengods

Get Day of the Vikings, an ARKANE thriller
by J.F.Penn:www.jfpenn.com/free

* * *

Day of the Vikings, an ARKANE thriller

A ritual murder on a remote island under the shifting skies of the aurora borealis.

A staff of power that can summon Ragnarok, the Viking apocalypse.

When Neo-Viking terrorists invade the British Museum in London to reclaim the staff of Skara Brae, ARKANE agent Dr. Morgan Sierra is trapped in the building along with hostages under mortal threat.

As the slaughter begins, Morgan works alongside psychic Blake Daniel to discern the past of the staff, dating back to islands invaded by the Vikings generations ago.

Can Morgan and Blake uncover the truth before Ragnarok is unleashed, consuming all in its wake?

Day of the Vikings is a fast-paced, supernatural thriller set in London and the islands of Orkney, Lindisfarne and Iona. Set in the present day, it resonates with the history and myth of the Vikings.

If you love an action-packed thriller,
you can get Day of the Vikings for free now:

WWW.JFPENN.COM/FREE

Day of the Vikings features Dr. Morgan Sierra from the ARKANE thrillers, and Blake Daniel from the London Crime Thrillers, but it is also a stand-alone novella that can be read and enjoyed separately.

AUTHOR'S NOTE

From J.F.Penn:

I'M BRITISH, BUT I lived in New Zealand for seven years and I hold a New Zealand passport. I support the All Blacks at rugby, even when they're playing England, and I'm married to a Kiwi. I've traveled all over the North and South Islands and experienced the wonders that they offer to adventurers. So I love New Zealand, and I hope that my passion for the country comes through in this story.

You can see some of the pictures that inspired the book, including my own images at: www.pinterest.com/jfpenn/risen-gods/

When I first arrived in Auckland back in 2000, I traveled north. I dived the Poor Knights Islands and visited Tane Mahuta in the Waipoua Forest. Then I went south, camping by the mud pools in Rotorua, and I also hiked the Tongariro Crossing. That steaming landscape was used for Mordor in *Lord of the Rings*. My fascination with the Pacific Rim of Fire began then and, although I wasn't in

Christchurch when the 2011 earthquakes hit, I had friends there. So this story has been percolating for years and I'm thrilled it's finally made it out into the world.

I've kept the landscape as real as possible, although distances have been shortened for the sake of speeding up the story sometimes. I've also tried to respect the Maori people, culture and customs in the book but of course, it is fiction, and should be taken as such. Maori traditions are primarily oral and differ by *iwi*, or tribe. All are similar in that they are holistic, entwining the earth and people with the spiritual realm, but there are differences in interpretation.

The following books were used for research:

Legends of Aotearoa by Chris Winitana and Andy Reisinger

Land of the Long White Cloud: Maori Myths, Tales and Legends by Kiri Te Kanawa

Maori Tales and Legends Collected and Retold by Kate McCosh Clark

GLOSSARY OF MAORI AND NEW ZEALAND WORDS

We have attempted to use Te Reo – the Maori language – in appropriate ways throughout the book. Here are the words used and if any are wrong, we apologize for any errors. The use of the macron for long vowels, e.g. 'a' in Māori, was considered but the decision was made to omit it so as not to confuse international readers with pronunciation.

Aotearoa - originally used as a reference to the North Island, now widely recognized as the Maori name for the country of New Zealand

Hangi - traditional Maori way of cooking food on heated rocks buried in a pit oven

Hapu - extended family, comprised of a number of whanau

Hawaiki - traditional Maori place of origin

Hokioi - huge mythical birds of prey

Hongi - traditional Maori greeting where the nose and forehead are pressed together so the breath of life is intermingled

Iwi - tribe, set of people bound together by a common ancestor

Kai moana - seafood

Kaitiaki - a guardian spirit

Karakia - prayers, incantations

Kaumatua - tribal elder

Kia ora - greeting; hello, be well

Koru - the unfurling frond of the silver fern. A Maori symbol of creation and new life.

Manaia - mythical creature with the head of a bird and the body of a man. The messenger between the physical world and the domain of the spirits, used as a guardian against evil.

Marae - meeting ground, a fenced complex of carved buildings and grounds, the focal point of Maori community

Moko - Maori tattoos

Motuhake - special

Pakeha - Maori name for white, non-Maori New Zealanders

Papatuanuku - goddess of the earth. Together with Ranginui, one of the primordial gods from the creation myth

Pounamu - greenstone, nephrite jade

Rakahore - god of rock and stone

Ranginui - god of the sky

Rarohenga - the underworld and realm of the spirits

Raukawa Moana - sea of bitter leaves. Maori name for the Cook Strait.

Ruaumoko - god of earthquakes and volcanoes

Taiaha - traditional weapon; a staff made of wood or whalebone

Tane Mahuta - Lord of the Forest; a specific ancient kauri tree in Northland

Tangaroa - god of the sea

Tangata whenua - people of the land, Maori name for themselves

Tangihanga or tangi - funeral rite held on the marae

Taniwha - supernatural creature that protects certain physical places

Taonga - ancestral treasure

Tawhirimatea - god of storms and the weather

Te Parata - a monster of the tidal ocean who caused the high and low tides by swallowing vast quantities of water and then spitting it out again

Te Reo - Maori language

Te Rerenga Wairua - the leaping-off place where the spirits of the dead enter the underworld. Cape Reinga, the northern tip of New Zealand

Te Wharenui - the meeting house on the marae

Te Wheke-a-Muturangi - mythical monstrous octopus

Toroa - albatross

Tui - a New Zealand honeyeater bird with a distinctive call

Tumatauenga - the red-faced god of war

Waka - oceangoing canoes

Waka wairua - a spirit canoe

Whakapapa - genealogy, ancestry

Whanau - extended family

Whiro - god of darkness and embodiment of evil

Other New Zealand terms/slang

Banana bread - particularly yummy banana cake often eaten for breakfast with butter

Lemon and Paeroa - fizzy drink made in Paeroa, a town in the North Island

Moro bar - chocolate bar with nougat and caramel

Number 8 wire - New Zealand term that implies a can-do attitude and the ability to fix anything

She'll be right - New Zealand slang meaning 'everything will be OK.'

Sweet as - New Zealand slang for good, cool, awesome

Tiki tour - scenic tour; a roundabout way of getting somewhere

If you enjoy **dark fantasy,** check out:

Map of Shadows, Mapwalkers #1
Risen Gods
American Demon Hunters: Sacrifice

A Thousand Fiendish Angels:
Short stories based on Dante's Inferno

The Dark Queen

More books by J. Thorn

Browse J. Thorn's entire catalog at
www.jthorn.net/books

ABOUT J.F.PENN

J.F.Penn is the Award-nominated, New York Times and USA Today bestselling author of the ARKANE supernatural thrillers, London Crime Thrillers, and the Mapwalker dark fantasy series, as well as other standalone stories.

Her books weave together ancient artifacts, relics of power, international locations and adventure with an edge of the supernatural. Joanna lives in Bath, England and enjoys a nice G&T.

* * *

You can sign up for a free thriller,
Day of the Vikings, and updates from behind the scenes, research, and giveaways at:

WWW.JFPENN.COM/FREE

* * *

Connect at:
www.JFPenn.com
joanna@JFPenn.com
www.Facebook.com/JFPennAuthor
www.Instagram.com/JFPennAuthor
www.Twitter.com/JFPennWriter

* * *

For writers:

Joanna's site, www.TheCreativePenn.com, helps people write, publish and market their books through articles, audio, video and online courses.

She writes non-fiction for authors under Joanna Penn and has an award-nominated podcast for writers, The Creative Penn Podcast.

ABOUT J. THORN

J. Thorn is a Top 100 Most Popular Author in Horror, Science Fiction, Action & Adventure and Fantasy (Amazon Author Rank). He has published two million words and has sold more than 185,000 books worldwide. In March of 2014 Thorn held the #5 position in Horror alongside his childhood idols Dean Koontz and Stephen King (at #4 and #2 respectively). He is an official member of the Science Fiction and Fantasy Writers of America, the Horror Writers Association, and the Great Lakes Association of Horror Writers.

Thorn earned a B.A. in American History from the University of Pittsburgh and a M.A. from Duquesne University. He is a full-time writer, part-time professor at John Carroll University, co-owner of Molten Universe Media, podcaster, FM radio DJ, musician, and a certified Story Grid nerd.

Get a free dark fantasy trilogy from J. Thorn:
http://bit.ly/risengods

ACKNOWLEDGEMENTS

Thanks to Jen Blood for great editing and to Wendy Janes for proofreading. Thanks to Jane Dixon Smith for cover design and interior print formatting.

The map of New Zealand/Aotearoa was designed by Brianne Ryan www.brianneryan.com

Thanks to Aaron Compton for reading and giving feedback from a Maori perspective and to Jonathan Byron for reading from a geologist and vulcanologist perspective.

J. Thorn would like to thank all of the readers who continue to support him in this crazy endeavor.

J.F.Penn would like to thank all her readers, especially the Pennfriends and the listeners at The Creative Penn podcast.